THE PIE-RATS OF THE CARIBBEAN

CARIBBEAN

DEE'S MYSTERY SOLVERS

LEONARD D. HILLEY II

Cover by Ellie Douglas. Custom Covers available: https://www.authorellie.com/covers

For Christal, my wonderful children, and my grandkids
A special thanks to KC Riley-Gyer and Ellie Douglas

CHAPTER

ONE

T he strange portal led the Mystery Solvers to a narrow dark tunnel that opened beneath a long pier. The opening was small, causing the four of them to hunch over and duck walk where the boards of the pier met the rocky supports.

Soft, gentle waves sloshed and splashed against the rocks and the timber support poles. The sharp mews of seagulls came outside the tunnel. Mists of saltwater carried a fishy smell and in the far distance the laughs and happy squeals of people suggested they were near a beach.

"Where are we?" Dee whispered. While crouched beneath the pier, she cautiously glanced at the bright water reflecting the early morning sunrise. The rippling water was blinding to behold directly with the sun's intensity, so she shielded her eyes with her hand.

Marty shrugged. "We have no way to know without looking, and squatting down like this at my height is causing my legs to burn. We need to see where we are. The chambers inside the portal don't foretell any destination. We could end up anywhere or in another realm or in a place we've already been."

Dee shook her head. "I don't remember this place."

Lynn gripped Marty's hand tightly. "Nor I. That's what worries me the most."

Marty nodded. "I know. I'm always uncomfortable passing through the portal, but my curiosity gets the best of me."

"I know," Dee said. "Isn't it excitingly *cool*?"

Adam voice quaked from his slight fear of uncertainty. "I thought you were mapping the portal doors in the cavern."

Dee said, "We tried, remember? Even the places we deemed safe and wanted to return to were different when we reentered. Only a few of them allowed us to return to the same place. It's like playing roulette or bingo."

"Yep," Marty nodded. "Each time we're taking a chance."

"I know," Adam replied softly. "It'd not be so nerve-racking if we had some idea where we were going."

"Some adventures are best when we don't know what to expect," Dee said.

"They can also be more deadly," Adam said. "What if we hit some sort of abnormal loop that prevented us from ever getting home?"

"That's a possibility," Dee said.

Lynn shivered, despite the heat. "Don't say things like that. I don't want to imagine how awful it'd be not being able to get home."

Marty held Lynn's hand and duck-walked toward the faint light outside. Even before they reached the brighter light, Lynn's pale skin made her almost glow in the dimness and her jet-black hair seemed invisible.

"I'll lead the way," Marty said. "We need to make certain we remember where this pier is. Otherwise, we could lose our way to go home."

Dee said, "From the looks of it, this won't be hard to find again."

"We need to hurry," Lynn said. "My mother's supposed to pick me up this evening at your grandparents. You know how she is about my whereabouts. If I'm not there—"

Dee pressed the button on her phone and to her surprise, she actually had bars. "Wow."

"What is it?" Lynn asked.

"We're somewhere in our world," she said with a bit of relief in her voice.

Lynn shook her head. "Can't you be a little more specific?"

"Unfortunately, no." Dee grinned and held her phone toward Lynn. "But look. I have service. You could text your mother and ask to stay another night or two if necessary."

"I doubt she'd go for that, even though we have no actual plans together," Lynn said. "But, it's worth a shot. What should I tell her?"

Marty said, "You could tell her that Grandpa needs more hands for the chores on the farm."

Lynn texted a long message. "But what if she makes a surprise visit and checks?"

Dee grinned. "She's never done that before, right?"

Lynn rolled her eyes and shook her head. "When has she *not*? She does even when I'm at your house, and we live on the same street. I swear she'd keep me on a leash if laws permitted it."

"She's a bit overbearing, I agree," Dee said. The sea breeze teased her sandy-blonde, bobbed hair, which almost glistened in the sunlight.

"A *bit*?" Lynn smiled wryly.

Dee giggled. "Okay, she's a *lot* overbearing. But you're going to be a junior this year and you turn eighteen before we graduate next year. That should grant you some—"

"Are you kidding?" Lynn said. "I can only see it getting worse. I picture my wedding day ending like this: She'll drive me to my honeymoon destination and have an adjoining hotel room."

Dee burst into a fit of laughter and couldn't breathe.

"Sure, laugh," Lynn said. "She's feared the empty nest since I was three. Possibly earlier than that. So, like I said, she'll probably want me home this evening."

"Yeah, yeah," Dee said, catching her breath and fanning her face with her hand. "Marty and I need to return home, too, because our mother wants us to go to some festival in Ravenswood. Not that I *want* to go, and being late might get us in trouble, but it'd save me from having to go. I wish we had a decent excuse *not* to go."

"Well," Lynn said. "Perhaps you should text her, too, eh? Besides, your mother's not as strict as mine."

"Or mine," Adam said.

"Phht," Dee said. "Adam, your mother seldom checks on your whereabouts, *ever*."

Adam huffed. "Gee, thanks for reminding me."

The sadness in his voice caused Dee quick remorse. "Sorry, Adam. I didn't mean it to sound like that."

"Eh, don't worry about it," he said, adjusting his ball cap. "It's true."

"Yeah, but still—"

"It's okay, Dee."

"In some ways," Dee said, "I wish Marty and I had a mother with less intrusive oversight. You're lucky she doesn't keep constant track of your whereabouts."

"If you say so," Adam said.

"She's not kidding," Lynn said. "My mother's worse than theirs and all of you know it. Instead of getting better as I grew up, she became more obsessive of what I was doing at all times. She smothers me with unnecessary attention. I'm surprised she hasn't bugged my shoes with a GPS tracker or implanted one under my skin."

Adam stared at her shoes. "You might consider checking them to see."

"Not a bad idea."

Metal crunched under Marty's shoe as he stepped farther away from the portal door camouflaged in the rocky beach wall that supported the long pier.

"What was that?" Dee asked.

"Not sure," Marty said. "I've stepped on several, flimsy metal objects so far. Probably aluminum cans someone tossed after drinking."

Coming into the daylight, they found themselves on a beach with white sand. The water was a transparent turquoise.

"Where are we?" Dee said in a hushed tone.

"I don't know," Lynn said. "But it's beautiful."

They climbed up to the pier and were on the east side of the T-shaped pier. Marty pointed. "Dee's right. We're still in our world. There's a cruise ship."

"Wow," Adam said in awe.

"Oh my," Dee whispered. "This is so-o-o exciting. I'm glad we packed swimsuits in our packs, Lynn."

"And sunscreen," Lynn said, eyeing Adam fiercely before he could make a snide, teasing comment about her pale complexion.

Adam raised his hands upward in surrender and half-grinned. "Hey, wasn't going to say a thing." He motioned an X across his chest. "I swear."

"Good," Lynn said with a fierce nod.

"We don't have time for the beach," Marty said. "We need to find out where we are first."

"Aww," Dee said. "Don't ruin the fun before we even get a chance to start."

"Dee, our first objective is to know where we are, stick together, and then we might be able to spend a half hour on the beach."

"A half hour?" Lynn and Dee said in harmony.

"The heck with any curfew," Dee said. "I'd like to spend an entire week here."

Lynn nodded. "The same."

Adam turned his ball cap backwards and grinned. "I may never go back. It's not like my mother's going to be looking for me."

"Look, as much as I like to be on the beach, too," Marty said, "we must keep in mind that we still don't know how long the portal door will be there. It could vanish and we'd be stuck here."

"At the moment, I'm not seeing a negative with that," Adam said.

"I hate to admit it, brother," Dee said, "but you're right. Our parents would be worried sick—again. And Papaw would find himself being interrogated by our mother, even though he doesn't know where we are. But, if she managed to squeeze the information about the portal out of him, we'd all face severe consequences unlike anything before. I hate when our mother chews Papaw out."

"He's put himself on the line for all of us several times," Lynn said. "Once you find out where we are, maybe text him?"

Dee bit her upper lip and nodded. "Not a bad idea."

Marty pointed. "We could ask that couple where we are."

Dee chuckled.

"What?" Marty asked.

"We're not exactly dressed like beachgoers."

"That's true," Marty said. "We need to find a place with restrooms so we can change into more appropriate clothes, but I'll asked them anyway."

The young couple, in their early twenties, were holding hands and leaning against one another while they walked. The lovesick gazes they exchanged with one another could only be from a couple who were on their honeymoon, or at least, that was the view Dee fantasized.

Marty said, "Excuse me. Can you tell me where we're at?"

The couple stared at one another with confusion and their expressions indicated they realized how out of place the Mystery Solvers were. Since the portal they used to teleport to other places was through an underground cavern system, they dressed in warm clothes and packed a variety of clothing to wear once they determined the climate on the other side of the portal.

The man looked at the Mystery Solvers' clothing, frowned, and said, "You're lost?"

"Kinda," Marty said.

"You're in Ocho Rios at the port," he said. "This is Jamaica. Did you get off a cruise ship?"

Marty didn't seem to know how to answer. Dee could see him struggling for the right words to explain why they were dressed in spelunking clothes.

"Yes," Dee said with her cellphone in hand. "Yesterday. We were trying to explore and looking for some butterflies to take pictures of. Time sort of got away from us."

"Ah, I'd say. Time does seem to stand still here," the young woman said with a broad smile. "That also explains your clothes."

"Yeah," Dee said. "We're going to go change. So Ocho Rios?"

"Yes," the man said with a curious smile. "In Jamaica. But, if you arrived on a cruise ship, you should know—"

"Sorry to have troubled you," Marty said, grabbing Lynn by the hand and hurrying past.

"Oh, no problem at all," he replied. His expression remained confused.

After the couple walked away, Lynn and Dee formed fists and shook them vigorously while jumping up and down before squealing, "We're in Jamaica!"

Marty rolled his eyes and shook his head. "Come on. Let's go find a place to change clothes."

CHAPTER
TWO

The Mystery Solvers changed clothes in the terminal restrooms where the cruise ship pier joined. Marty and Adam wore khaki shorts and button-down Hawaiian shirts and flip-flops. Dee and Lynn wore one piece bathing suits with swimsuit coverups, even though they weren't certain they get to go to the beach.

Lynn applied some eyeliner and mascara while she and Dee were in the restroom. Once she stepped into the sunlight, she appeared goth or someone trying to represent The Day of the Dead.

"Anyone else getting hungry?" Dee asked.

Adam nodded. "I could eat ... a LOT."

"I think we all could," Marty said. "But the food vendors here are swamped. Maybe we could find a small restaurant or pie shop nearby."

"Pie?" Adam licked his lips. "I'm for that. Pie would be even better."

Dee grinned. "I'd love to try a cinnamon pie."

Lynn scrunched her nose. "Cinnamon? Sounds harsh."

"I hear it's delicious," Dee said.

"I'd rather have Key-lime," Lynn said.

"Both sound great to me," Adam said. "I'm so hungry, I could eat a slice of each."

Marty laughed. "We're not going to get either if we don't find a place to eat. Remember, our time is limited today."

"It's a shame, too," Dee said, as they exited the terminal and walked toward the downtown section of the city. "There are so many places I'd love to stop and shop."

"The air, breeze, and the sound of the sea and birds," Lynn said. "I hope we get to return again one day for a longer period of time."

Dee glanced at Marty while he held Lynn's hand. His mind seemed focused on the same beauty Lynn had mentioned and his hand tightened on hers.

"This place would be perfect for a wedding or honeymoon," Marty half whispered.

Dee's and Adam's mouths dropped. Lynn blushed and her eyes widened slightly as she gazed at Marty. His face reddened, and Dee wondered if he'd meant to say the words out loud at all. Had he absently allowed his thoughts to be spoken?

Adam looked at Dee with a wide-eyed expression. Dee shrugged.

Marty had turned eighteen only six weeks earlier, but she and Lynn and Adam were all still sixteen, but Lynn was closer to turning seventeen than Adam or Dee.

Marty and Lynn had dated for almost two years, and Marty debated on going away to college before Lynn graduated from high school. Although he hadn't asked Lynn about marriage since she was underage, they were inseparable and seemed destined to wed sometime in the future. Was his comment a subtle hint he planned to ask her hand in marriage soon?

Marty held a sheepish expression and exchanged occasional glances with Lynn as they walked. His statement had made the situation a bit awkward and none of them knew how to further the conversation.

The four stopped at several shops along the way. A lot of these places sold art and a couple had carved wood art that was remarkable and detailed in such a fashion that Dee couldn't stop staring at the etched carvings. Their skills were probably unmatched. They browsed several straw hat shops and stores that sold various clothing and souvenirs. All the vendors were friendly, smiled, and greeted them, offering to help with any questions they might have. Knowing they didn't have anywhere to tote a lot of items and take them through the portal, they bought little.

Dee and Lynn both bought straw hats to help reduce the chance of getting sunburned. Adam bought several key rings and a T-shirt. Marty secretly purchased a shell necklace while Lynn wasn't paying attention, but his gift didn't escape Dee's eyes, who prided herself for being ever watchful and a great detective.

After an hour of exploring the shops, they finally came upon a small pie shop: Kiyana's Pie Shop. They peered through the window. Only two round tables with four chairs each were near the door. Six tall, swivel stools were fastened to the floor at the counter beside a glass case with pie shelves.

Adam's stomach growled. Dee and Lynn laughed.

"What?" he asked. "I told you I was starving."

Dee pointed and said, "How about that place? We could get pie or coffee or sandwiches, according to the outside chalkboard menu sign."

Marty grinned and released an obvious sigh of relief. "It's as good a place as any."

CHAPTER
THREE

The aroma of fresh baked pies permeated the inside of the small shop. Dee's mouth watered. She'd never smelled anything so delicious that she almost drooled. She hurried to the glass display case to select a piece of pie and hoped they had cinnamon.

She groaned.

The shelves inside the pie case were empty, except for some large crumbs and an occasional pie chunk. A few empty pie tins were flipped over and some of the fruity pie fillings was smeared on the inside of the glass and smudges were everywhere. It almost appeared like a food fight had taken place *inside* the case.

The lady behind the counter was busy putting mixing bowls into the large industrial sink. Her thick braided hair was wrapped into a beautiful bun, and its length was still impressively long. Her white apron was soiled with unbleached flour, egg yolks, and various spices. Pinned to the front of the apron was a name tag with 'Kiyana' printed on it.

Dee was excited to see the shop's owner. Kiyana greeted Dee with a broad, but tired, smile.

"Wow!" Dee said with her hands pressed against the display's front glass. She gave Kiyana a disappointed stare. "No pies?"

"Not yet. Dey're baking," Kiyana said, in a thick accent. "Should be ready in 'bout a half hour."

"Wow," Lynn said. "You must sell a lot of pies."

"You'd think," Kiyana said with a disappointed expression. "But, no. We used to bake pies da day before and den, keep them locked inside the display for the next morning. But, as you see, they disappear overnight. We no longer fill the case with pies at night. Maybe only three pies were left yesterday. And, I still gotta clean the case before I can set fresh pies inside. At dis rate, I'll be outta business before the month's out."

Dee whispered to Lynn, "I love her accent."

Lynn smiled and nodded.

"So this isn't the first time the pies have disappeared?" Dee asked, taking out a small notepad and black pen.

"Uh, no," Kiyana replied. "It's gone on ... three months now."

Marty frowned. "But the case has a lock on it."

"Ah, yes, it does," Kiyana said. She shrugged, sighed, and wiped her hands with a damp towel. "But, it make no difference. Each morning we arrive and find de pies gone, with everything strewn around inside, but the case is still locked. Tis mystery, if ya ask me."

Adam whispered, "I never thought I'd see the need to lock pies up. Unless, they're that delicious."

Dee smiled.

"What?" Kiyana said. "Ya find dis funny?"

Dee quickly shook her head and retracted her smile. "No, not at all. It's just ... we solve a lot of mysteries back home."

"And Dee here," Lynn said, "*loves* mysteries. Just the mention of the word and she lights up, like now. See?"

"Ah, yes, I see," Kiyana said. "And ya think dat ya can solve dis one, eh?"

"We could try," Dee replied.

Marty shook his head and whispered, "We don't have time."

Dee frowned at him. "We have at least enough time to determine if we can help Kiyana find the culprits."

Marty sighed.

Dee beamed a triumphant smile.

Lynn gritted her teeth. "There goes the beach."

Looking at Kiyana, Marty said, "No surveillance cameras?"

"Are ya kidding, young man? I can't afford such technology. I barely make ends meet as is. And now, a thief helping himself to me pies every day." She shook her head in frustration. Tears formed in her eyes.

"Any clues?" Dee asked.

"None I've noticed. None the police have found," Kiyana said. She blotted tears with a paper napkin. "Sorry. It's so infuriating. A couple of detectives watched the place for a few nights. Each morning, the pies were still gone. Officers said dat they saw no one ever enter or leave."

Dee's lips formed a tight smile. Then, her eyes brightened. "The four of us are private detectives back home."

"You?" Kiyana asked. "Aren't ya a bit young to be solving crimes?"

"Actually," Dee said. "We've done quite well for ourselves. With your permission, do you mind if we look for clues?"

Kiyana smiled apologetically. "I can't afford to hire you."

"We understand," Dee said. "Perhaps, if we solve the case, you could pay us with a cinnamon pie?"

Kiyana studied Dee for several seconds. She nodded, grinned broadly despite her tears, and extended her hand. "Now, *dat* I could do."

Dee shook Kiyana's hand with more enthusiasm than Kiyana expected. The shop owner's eyes widened from a sense of rising hope and appreciation.

"Key-lime would be better," Lynn grumbled.

"I could do both, provided ya catch da thief," Kiyana said.

Marty said, "Does anyone else have a key to your front door?"

"No," Kiyana replied. "And no one except me has one to da alleyway door where da dumpsters are, either. Do me a favor, young lady, flip the open sign over on da door. No sense having any more disappointed customers coming in."

Lynn walked to the door and flipped the open sign to closed.

"Is it okay if we come behind the counter to look for clues?" Dee asked.

"Ah, help yourselves," she said, "but don't get in da way, and be mindful of the hot stove and pans. I give you an hour. No more. By den, some of the pies should be ready, and I need to wait on customers."

"That works," Dee said, rubbing her hands together.

"Dee," Marty whispered. "You know we don't have much time before we need to go home."

Dee frowned. "I know, but how hard can it be?"

Adam sighed and rolled his eyes.

Lynn groaned with an agitated frown.

"What?" Dee said.

"Every time you say that, Sis, we get into some serious trouble," Marty said. "I've taken blame for some things I shouldn't have, just to keep you from getting grounded."

"You're a great big brother," Dee said, smiling and patting his back. "Shouldn't we at least check it out?"

Marty shook his head. "We don't know these streets or who might be stealing the pies."

Dee huffed. "That's why we investigate, silly."

"Please listen to Marty," Adam said.

Slightly hurt, Dee glanced at Lynn. "You want to turn against me, too, Lynn?"

"It's not a matter of *want*," Lynn said. "I'd rather collect some seashells or look around the shops instead. Some cool things I'd like to buy. Besides, I wouldn't have put on my swimsuit and tons of greasy sunscreen if I thought we weren't *going* to the beach."

"Sorry," Dee said softly. "We'll be quick, okay? How cool would it be to solve a mystery in the Caribbean?"

"The beach would be cooler," Lynn said.

Adam frowned. "It's actually pretty humid outside."

Lynn glared at him. Adam shrugged.

"Cool, maybe, but who could you tell, Dee?" Marty said. "If Mom ever finds out—"

Dee sighed. "I know. It'd be our secret. At least for now. But still it'd be something we'd know we did."

"All right," Marty said. "Let's look for clues."

CHAPTER
FOUR

Marty followed Dee to the other side of the glass pie case. Though he was against Dee's decision, he knew it was easier to placate than argue. The quicker she realized they couldn't find the thief, the quicker they could hit the beach and then go home. Sometimes he wished the portal had never opened, and yet, he wondered why it had. In an odd way, from what Grandpa had told them, they seemed destined to discover what lie beyond their world.

Grandpa had seen numerous, unexplainable things when he had been their age, and he had shared a few of those experiences with them, but Marty knew his grandfather had held back in telling everything he knew. Some things were too dangerous to encounter and because of that, his grandfather had kept secrets about the farm. A *lot* of secrets.

He suspected the portal and the mysterious creatures and events Grandpa had seen was probably why the National Guard had built a small base right beside the farm. The base had been established only twenty years earlier. Marty and Dee's mother had mentioned that the National Guard had tried numerous times to buy Grandpa's farm, but he held firm and denied every offer. In Marty's mind, this meant only one thing. Grandpa knew about the portal, and now, Marty suspected the military had somehow learned about it, especially after the alien and UFO.

Marty knelt behind the pie case and noticed some odd footprints at the edge of the case. What appeared to be mud, he soon learned was not. He ran his finger across the footprint and sniffed. Chocolate?

"Hmm," he said softly.

Dee peered over his shoulder. "Did you find something?"

He shrugged. "What do you make of that footprint?"

She squinted. "Wow. It looks like a shoe print for an action figure or something similar. I wonder if Kiyana has any children who play with dolls here?"

"You could ask. If not, it's weird," Marty said. He looked at the scuffed markings on the bottom of the padlock. "Someone has picked the lock. Maybe several times."

"How can you tell?"

"I guess someone could've used a key," Marty said, holding the lock. "But usually one doesn't miss the keyhole so often to scrape deep etches like that."

"That is odd," Dee said.

Lynn and Adam searched the aluminum tables and shelves at opposite sides of the kitchen.

Dee crouched beside Marty and peered under the pie case. "This place could use a good cleaning."

"Ah, could it now?" Kiyana asked in passing while carrying a pan of steaming hot pies and setting them on an aluminum table. "I'll be gettin' to it soon enough."

Dee winced. "Sorry. I didn't mean—"

"Don't be sorry. Truth's the truth. It be like dis each morning—total mess—but since I can't afford to hire help, I do what I can do. I sweep and mop while de pies cool."

Dee waited until Kiyana headed back to the stove and whispered, "Lots of pie crumbs and loose filling under the case."

Marty chuckled and shook his head. "Who'd take the time to eat stolen pie inside the shop?"

"A hungry thief," Dee said with a broad grin.

"And how did crumbs get that far beneath the case?" Marty asked.

"Maybe he or she kicked the crumbs under there. But one would have to be awful hungry to—"

Marty grinned. "Eat and run?"

She snickered. "It gives a new meaning to the phrase, huh?"

"If, as you say, the person could be hungry and couldn't wait to eat ... Or it's someone who doesn't care to get caught or thinks he can't get caught. Do you see anything else under there?"

Dee squinted. "Um. Well ... looks like more little shoe prints."

"Seriously?"

"Would I lie about that?"

"I'm not saying you're lying. It's just even *weirder*."

Dee stood and smiled. "With all the things we've seen? Really, big bro? The portal has opened up all sorts of things we never thought we'd see."

"That's true," Marty replied. "You think, maybe, gnomes?"

Dee's brow creased, and she pursed her lips. "Well, I *wasn't*. Now that you mention it, is it all that unlikely? We have seen dwarves and pixies and sprites. Or you ... you can see ghosts."

Marty waved his hand and stood. "Let's not even go there."

"You don't know how much I envy you," Dee said.

"About seeing ghosts?"

"No. Of us four, you're the only one who could stay here without worrying about Mom's curfew," Dee said. "The rest of us have two more years of high school."

Marty sighed. "I know, but don't be envious of that."

Dee frowned. "Why not?"

"Sis, I graduated, but with the rest of you in school, it makes me miss high school even more."

Dee nodded. "I understand that. You said that you're not going to college yet, so what will you do?"

"I plan to help Grandpa around the farm several days each week, and the other days, I'll keep working and saving money," Marty said. "Come on. Let's see if Lynn and Adam found anything."

"What are we going to do about the footprints?" Dee asked.

"We'll come back to them in a few minutes. It's doubtful the prints go far, but maybe they'll led us in the right direction."

CHAPTER
FIVE

Lynn searched the right side of the kitchen, and looked around the tables and shelves for clues. She didn't put a lot of focus on the hunt for evidence, as she'd rather be on the beach with Marty. Besides, the thick sunscreen made her skin itch, which was why she hated wearing it and wished she'd have waited until she knew for certain they were going to the beach. With her pale skin condition, she could never tan and would always be alabaster white. The sun was often her worst enemy and whenever she felt embarrassed or angered, her skin reddened bright like a windblown, burning piece of coal.

Thinking about what Marty had said about Jamaica being a great place for a wedding and honeymoon, she blushed. Her face heated, and her stomach twisted with excitement. She wouldn't say the sensation felt like fluttering *butterflies* trapped in her stomach, but the analogy was close. Although they had been girlfriend and boyfriend for more than a year, they never really talked about what the future might hold for the two of them. She smiled. With the way she felt toward him and he toward her, no words had been necessary. They both seemed to know and understand they were destined to be together. While their parents were okay with them being together, they also stressed they were too young to understand life and the meaning of real commitment.

She giggled to herself. Most of the adults she knew, and even her mother, didn't understand life yet, either. But since her parents were no longer together, Lynn understood hardships came to everyone. Kids learned—whether for better or worse—from what they endured during their childhoods. The decision for how a child will live as an adult is strictly each person's choice. Since her mother had been overbearing and overprotective, Lynn decided she didn't want to treat her children in the same manner. She promised herself to be more lenient, and hoped she'd be able to keep that promise in the future.

Lynn understand there was no foolproof guide with all the answers for all situations. The unpredictability of life was what made living interesting, but no guarantees were ever given.

From the corner of her eye, she noticed Marty and Dee talking and pointing at the floor and under the pie case. Had they found something? If so, why were they obsessing about something *under* the pie case.

Lynn walked to them. "What did you find?"

Dee leaned closer and whispered, "Tiny shoe prints."

Lynn frowned. "How tiny?"

"Like a fashion doll," Dee replied.

"Seriously? Maybe some kids were playing in here with toys," Lynn said.

"Under the pie case?" Marty asked.

Lynn laughed. "That's not possible. What do you think?"

Dee grinned. "I'm thinking gnomes."

"Gnomes?" Lynn said. "They'd be too big to fit under there, silly."

Dee pointed at Marty. "Actually, Marty was the one who suggested it."

"Lynn, what's your opinion?" Marty asked.

"Not gnomes," she replied.

"Did you find anything, Lynn?" Dee asked.

"No. But, I wasn't looking *under* the shelves and tables."

"Okay," Marty said. "Let's look together."

The three of them began looking under the shelves and tables.

"There's a vent," Dee said.

Lynn squatted and observed. "Looks rather dirty, too."

Marty dropped to one knee and leaned through the shelf. "Looks like pie filling smeared around the edges of the vent cover. And the screws that would hold the cover in place are missing."

"Missing?" Dee's brow rose. "That's a pretty good sign we're dealing with an abnormally small thief."

Lynn crossed her arms and sighed. "Maybe, but I'd still rather be on the beach right now."

"I know," Dee sighed. "But, we're making progress."

"Hardly," Lynn said. "Let's say you're right, and some small creature's stealing pies. How are we going to go after them? Through there?"

"Of course not," Dee said.

"The vent has to lead outside," Marty said.

Lynn sighed. "At least that would get us out of here."

"Let's doublecheck everything we've found so far," Marty said.

Dee nodded. "That's a great idea. Maybe Adam found some clues."

"Adam?" Lynn said, rolling her eyes slightly.

"You never know," Dee said. "He might find a clue to lead us in the right direction."

CHAPTER
SIX

Adam turned his ball cap backwards and went into the stockroom. Bags of flour and sugar were neatly stacked on one set of shelves. Industrial sized cans of cherries, apples, and dates were set on slanted shelves for easier access beside a table with a heavy duty can opener. One gallon buckets of glaze and flavored icings were stacked on another rack of shelves. This was a paradise for those with a sweet tooth.

A large restaurant sink with a spray nozzle was beside the walk-in cooler and beside the cooler was a small, walk-in freezer.

He wasn't certain what to look for, as he expected the thief to exit whatever door he'd entered. But since Kiyana indicated that neither door had been used to get in or out of the pie shop, and no one else had any spare keys, how was this thief escaping notice?

Adam glanced at the ceiling. One of the tiles was slightly out of place. Being short in stature, he knew even with a ladder, he'd have a difficult time reaching the tile, and most likely, he couldn't. Attempting to stretch and reach the tile wasn't worth the risk. Marty was much taller, and would have an easier time inspecting the tile, so Adam decided to get him.

Adam left the stockroom and joined Dee, Marty, and Lynn, who were standing beside an aluminum table stocked with various sizes of bundt pans, muffin pans, and pie pans. He thought it strange they were looking through the pans and under the table.

"Uh," Adam said. "I think you guys should come look at this."

Dee turned her head sharply and her eyes widened with excitement. "You found a clue?"

He shrugged. "I'm not sure. Maybe. It might not be anything, but I can't reach it. I was hoping Marty could."

Marty stood and squared his shoulders slightly, which made him appear even taller. "Sure. Show me what you found."

In the stockroom, Adam pointed at the ceiling tile and explained how it looked off-center. "Maybe someone's tampered with it?"

Lynn frowned, showing her skepticism. "With what we found, I doubt the thief could even get up there."

Adam sighed with disappointment.

Marty patted Adam's shoulder. "Good eye. We need to check *anything* that could be a clue to find the thief. The quicker we get this done, the better. I'd like to go to the beach, too."

Adam smiled. "Thanks, Marty."

"Any clue is still a clue."

Adam glanced at Dee. "What did you all find?"

"Some very small shoe prints."

"Like a pixie?"

"Or something smaller," Dee said.

Lynn chuckled and shook her head. "They wanted to say it was gnomes, but gnomes are *too* large and bulky compared to smaller Fae."

Dee gave a disgruntled stare. "*Whatever* it is ... it's small enough to wear fashion doll-sized shoes or boots."

"O-o-h," Adam said. He strained to not roll his eyes, as he found the idea ridiculous.

Marty took an empty bucket and flipped it over. He climbed upon the bucket and pushed the ceiling tile upward. He peered inside.

"What'cha find?" Dee asked.

Marty coughed and grimaced. "Lots of dust and cobwebs."

"Aww," she said, shaking her head.

Adam sighed.

"And a piece of old pie crust," Marty said. "Look at this!"

He tossed a small doll-sized black boot to the floor.

Dee picked it up and frowned. "Why would it be up there?"

"Who knows? It was wedged between the tile and its holder. It might've been left whenever this piece of pie was eaten. Nothing seems to have gone this way since, or that boot would've probably fallen to the floor," Marty said. "Could someone get me a napkin?"

Lynn took a napkin from a dispenser and stepped on tiptoe to hand it to him. "Why do you need a napkin?"

Marty scrunched his nose and said, "I don't want to touch the pie crust with my bare hands."

"Eww!" Dee said.

"Double *eww!*" Adam said with a higher tone of voice.

Lynn and Dee burst into laughter. Their faces reddened and they held their stomachs.

Adam frowned. "What?"

"You don't realize how girly you just sounded?" Dee asked.

He shrugged. "So? I was just playing along. Geez."

Marty gently repositioned the tile back into its proper place and stepped down with the piece of pie crust wrapped inside the paper napkin. He unwrapped the crust and all four of them examined it.

"Looks like rodent teeth," Marty said.

Adam nodded. "My hamster used to gnaw on all sorts of things and those are definitely similar teeth marks."

"But it doesn't explain this?" Lynn said, holding the tiny boot.

Joking, Adam said, "Maybe a rat wore it?"

None of them laughed, and each gave him a slight frown.

"Sorry." Adam shrugged. "Do you have any better suggestions?"

Dee sighed and then grinned, perhaps picturing a rat wearing boots. "Not at the moment."

Marty said, "I suggest we hold onto this old crust and I'd like to check the vent in the other room. Maybe we can figure out where it leads outside."

Dee smiled. "That's a good start."

SEVEN

Dee followed Marty to the table. She stepped near the wall, out of his way, while he lowered to his knees to see the vent cover.

"What do you think?" Dee asked.

Marty shook his head. "I don't know."

Kiyana stepped to the table with another tray of hot pies and eased them atop the silvery table. "How's ya investigation coming along, eh?"

Dee said, "We've found a couple of things, but not sure if they'll help you find your thief or not."

"What did ya find?"

"Well, um, first, let me ask if you have any children that play behind the counter?" Dee asked.

"Children?" Kiyana shook her head with a slight frown as she thought for a moment. "No. There be no children playing here. Why?"

"The first thing we found were some boot prints under the glass pie case," Dee said. "And they match the plastic boot Lynn's holding."

Lynn held the boot between her thumb and forefinger so Kiyana could see it.

"Ah, now. So?" Kiyana asked. "Ya think something that small is stealing me pies? Come on, now. Ya gotta be putting me on."

"No. That's not what I'm implying," Dee said. "We don't know yet who is taking the pies. We're just showing you what we've found. Now, this little boot was wedged in a ceiling tile in the stockroom. Above the tile, my brother found an old piece of pie crust with gnaw marks on it. From the looks of the crust, it's been there quite a while."

"Let me see dat," Kiyana said.

Marty showed her the crust.

Kiyana scrunched her nose with disgust. "Dat looks like a rat chewed on it. But, I've seen no rodents in dis place, and especially none dat would wear tiny little boots. I don't know what kind of mysteries ya solve back home, but—"

"They're actually pretty strange mysteries," Dee said.

Marty nodded. "If we told you about some of them you wouldn't believe us."

Kiyana said, "You be right about dat. I probably wouldn't believe ya. Just how strange were they?"

Lynn blushed. "Paranormal occurrences."

Kiyana gave her a shrewd stare. "Paranormal, eh? Boogiemen? Ghosts?"

"Sometimes, yes," Dee said with a slight smile. Saying it aloud to a stranger even sounded made-up to herself.

"Ah, things dat might wear those tiny little boots? Don't you see how busy I am," Kiyana said. "I don't have time to waste with silly fairytales."

"We're trying to help you," Dee said. "Nothing we've said has been a lie."

Kiyana's upper lip curled. Her eyes narrowed, and she pointed at the door. "Get out! Go waste someone else's time. *Not* mine."

"But—" Dee said.

Marty shook his head at Dee. "Come on, Dee. You tried."

"Listen to your brother," Kiyana said. Tears welled in her eyes, and Dee assumed they were the product of her anger and from her shop being robbed.

"Sorry," Dee said, walking to the shop door.

"Kiyana," Marty said. "Might I ask one question before we leave?"

Kiyana took a deep breath and held it. Her jaw tightened. With a narrowed gaze, she sighed and nodded.

"The vent on the wall behind that table," Marty said, pointing. "Do you know if it leads outside or into the cooling system on the roof?"

She shrugged. "I'm not sure. Why?"

"The screws that should hold the cover into place are missing."

Her eyes widened. "Dey are?"

Dee nodded.

"Yes," Marty said. "Look, I'm sorry you feel like we wasted your time, but believe me, Dee's suspicions have seldom been wrong. Anyway, we'll see ourselves out."

As they left the shop, Dee kept watch over her shoulder. After the shop door eased shut, Kiyana approached the table and crouched, studying the vent beneath the table. She stared for several seconds but didn't reach for the cover to check its looseness. With a worried expression, she placed her hand over her mouth and looked toward the door. Dee kept hoping Kiyana would hurry to the door with a change of attitude and ask them to continue looking for clues, but she didn't.

The Mystery Solvers walked down the sidewalk toward the alleyway beside the store.

Dee formed fists and shook her head. "Why did she get so angry?"

"Maybe she thinks we're making light of the situation," Lynn said.

"Maybe," Dee said. Her face heated from agitation.

"For what it's worth, Dee," Marty said, "this is why I never want others to know I can see ghosts. Whether or not a person believes ghosts exist, they don't want to let others know they believe in such a possibility."

"But why are people like that?" Dee asked.

"Mainly because people tease or shun those who confess what they saw. No one wants to be considered *crazy*."

Dee said, "I never really considered that. I'm sorry I keep hounding you to look for ghosts."

"Don't worry about it," Marty said, waving it off. "With Kiyana, though, I have the feeling she believes us but fears admitting it."

"Really?" Lynn asked.

Marty grinned and nodded.

Lynn said, "What makes you say that?"

"Her eyes revealed her hidden fear after we showed her the little boot and I told her about the missing vent cover screws," Marty said. "You didn't notice it?"

"To be honest," Dee said. "Her sudden outburst and change in her demeanor shocked me and made me a little angry. I was only trying to help, so I missed seeing her fear, at first. But after we went outside, I watched her inspect the vent cover. She was too frightened to actually touch it, though."

Lynn said, "Superstitions are common in the Caribbean."

"Really?" Adam asked.

"Yes," Lynn said. "They have been for hundreds of years."

"Hmm," Dee said. "Kiyana might be thinking about any type of small creature stealing her pies."

Adam snickered. "Maybe pirate rats?"

"I know you want to be amusing," Dee said. "But sometimes your humor is so over the top that no one laughs."

"You never know," Adam said. "A portal took us here. What else might've traveled through the portal?"

Marty said, "He has a point."

Dee frowned. "But pirate rats?"

"Pie-Rats!" Adam said with a chuckle.

"Sheesh," Lynn said.

"What? It's a cute play on words," Adam said glumly.

"I'll give you that," Dee said.

Adam forced a slight grin. "Thanks."

"Okay," Marty said. "We need to decide if we look further for the thieves or go to the beach."

"I'm for the beach," Lynn said. "Or the zip line. Or the Blue Hole. I read it's a fantastic place to see."

"Dee?"

"You guys can go to the beach," Dee said. She didn't like how things ended with Kiyana and wanted to redeem herself. "I want to look around some more."

"We can't split up, Dee," Marty said. "One for continuing and one for going to the beach. Adam? How about you?"

Adam's brow tightened and he adjusted his cap. "I'm curious as to what left the boot wedged in the ceiling tile and why those screws are missing. Only something the size of a rat or a mystical creature could travel through the vent. So, I'd like to at least search a little longer."

"Okay. Two for staying and one for the beach," Marty said.

Lynn made pleading eyes at Marty, and Dee cringed. No way her brother was about to side with his sister over his girlfriend.

"Well, brother," Dee said, slightly holding her breath and worrying about his answer. "What's your vote?"

He gave a reluctant look at Lynn. "I say we give this another half hour to forty-five minutes. If we find nothing else, it's the beach."

Lynn halfway pouted.

"But I'm still hungry," Adam said.

"We all are," Dee said. "Let's go to that food stand over there, grab something quick, and then come back to this alley."

Lynn, Marty, and Adam nodded.

CHAPTER
EIGHT

After eating jerk chicken and rice wraps, the Mystery Solvers returned to the alleyway beside Kiyana's shop. With the afternoon looming, the temperature increased. Sweat dripped off all of them.

Dee wiped her face with a napkin. "I guess you're glad you wore the sunscreen now, Lynn?"

Lynn nodded. "Except for the itching. And perhaps, I should've thought better about putting on makeup."

Lynn's eyeliner and mascara had run, making her look more goth than ever.

The alleyway, at least, was in the shade due to the angle of the building and the sun's position. A crude ladder was fastened to the side of the pie shop, but the ladder didn't touch the asphalt and was well out of Adam's reach, though the other three could possibly grab the first rung. Marty certainly could, but she didn't think it'd be necessary. Midway up the ladder was a square opening, about the same size as the vent cover inside the shop.

Marty pointed. "That might be where the vent comes out."

"Are you going to climb up there?" Adam asked.

"I'm the only one tall enough to reach the bottom rung."

"I don't know, Marty," Dee said.

"What? It's not that far up."

"That's not what I'm referring to," Dee said. "When we looked at the vent cover, it's quite small. The only mess we saw was the pie filling smudges on the outside."

"True," Lynn said. "I don't think a full-size pie could be taken through the vent, much less fit. A piece of pie, depending upon how large Kiyana cuts them, might not fit, either. Think of the mess that would be made trying to carry a pie across the floor."

"Right," Dee said. "Most of the mess was inside the pie case and beneath it. The footprints went the opposite direction."

"Hmm," Marty said. "You're right."

Adam said, "Maybe they come into the pie shop through the vent and have another route to the outside. No way something so small could've ever gotten an entire pie through the ceiling panel in the stock room."

Marty nodded. "The pie crust we found in the ceiling was only a small piece of a pie. That could be done."

"Yes," Adam said. "Which might explain why the little boot got wedged and left behind. Even a small piece of pie would require holding it with both forepaws."

Dee smiled. "Wow, Adam! Great reasoning. But, that's if it were a rat.""

Adam grinned and slightly blushed.

"Much better analysis than those jokes you keep trying to tell," Lynn said.

"Hey, it's good to have him in our club," Marty said. "He's learning. Keep up the good work."

"Thanks," Adam said. "Kiyana said that the detectives never saw anyone enter or leave the shop. So what if there is more than one thief? Rats seem the most logical culprits. They're social and could work as a team. They all come in through the vent, take the pies out a different direction, and only one exits through the vent."

"Why would one do that?" Lynn asked.

"To be the lookout," Adam said. "Maybe be a distraction if it needed to help the other Pie-Rats escape."

Lynn rolled her eyes. "And we're back to nonsense."

"No," Marty said. "What he says makes sense."

"I'm referring to him calling them, *Pie-Rats*," Lynn said.

Marty shrugged and chuckled. "I don't know. I kinda like it."

"It would take a team to move the pies, though," Dee said. "Kiyana never said how many pies were stolen last night, did she?"

Marty shook his head. "No, she didn't."

Dee sighed. "I'd go ask, but after how upset she became, I don't think it's a good idea."

"Probably not," Marty said.

"What if, let's say, there are four or five pies that were taken last night," Dee said. "How many rats would it take to carry one pie?"

Lynn said, "It'd depend on how much each pie weighed."

"Right," Marty said. "And since we don't what pies were taken, we can't rightly know. A creme pie would weigh less than a nut or fruit pie."

"We also don't know how many trips they make," Adam said.

"There are too many parameters," Marty said.

"With the mess inside the pie case," Dee said, "they might have eaten a lot of pie before carrying them out."

"They'd have had to keep the pies in the pie tins," Lynn said. "Otherwise, they'd have left a trail for others to follow."

Dee swallowed hard. "I hate to say it, but we need to talk to Kiyana again."

Marty frowned. "Are you sure that's a good idea?"

Dee shrugged and looked nervous. "No. But we need to know specifics if we're going to find the thieves."

"So you think there's more than one, now?" Lynn asked.

"With Adam's observations and postulates, we have enough

evidence to believe more than one individual is responsible," Dee replied.

Lynn narrowed her gaze at Adam. Adam's brow rose and he made a goofy grin.

"Come on," Dee said. "Let's see if Kiyana will let us ask a few more questions."

CHAPTER
NINE

Dee pushed the pie shop door inward. The bell chimed. Kiyana set a pie inside the pie case she had thoroughly cleaned.

"Forgive me, Kiyana," Dee said. "But if we could ask only a couple more questions?"

Kiyana slid the glass door shut and rested her elbows atop the case. "Ah, you're still trying to solve dis mystery, eh, even after I insisted you don't?"

"Yes."

"Ah, look," Kiyana said. "Perhaps I was a bit too harsh with ya earlier, but—"

"We understand," Dee said.

"I doubt dat you do, unless you were in my position. But no matter," Kiyana said. "I shouldn't have lost me temper with ya. In spite of dat, you still want to help. So ask away. I'm almost ready for customers."

"On average," Dee said, "how many pies are left in the pie case at night?"

Kiyana shrugged. "Last night, there be three pies left. Starting tonight, though, I'm putting the extras in the walk-in fridge."

Marty said, "That's a good idea."

"So only three pies?" Dee asked.

"Yes. Dat might not seem like much, but think about price per slice instead of the number of pies. Three pies equals thirty-six slices, so my loss adds up quickly," Kiyana said.

"No doubt about it," Marty said.

"What about the pie tins? Did the tins disappear with the pies?" Adam asked.

"Yes, why?"

"What size are the pies?" Marty asked.

"Most pies are twenty to twenty-three centimeters," she replied. "Why?"

"How much do they weigh?" Marty asked.

"Between one and two kilograms," she replied.

Adam looked at Marty and Dee.

"That'd be between eight and nine inches," Marty said. "And nearly three pounds."

Dee said, "There's no way they'd fit through the vent."

Adam waved his fist in the air. "I knew it. There has to be another way out."

Kiyana gave Adam an odd stare. "Wait, he's still talking about small creatures stealing the pies?"

"Yes," Marty said. "And from earlier, you know something's coming through the vent. You failed to hide your suspicions when I mentioned it."

"And I saw you check the vent," Dee said, "after we left. You know, don't you?"

Embarrassed, Kiyana glanced at the floor and said, "Every now and den, I hear scratchy noises and have seen reddish eyes staring through the vent cover near closing time."

"And what do you think they are?" Dee asked.

"They look like rats," she replied. She visibly shivered.

Adam shook his fist again. "Yes!"

Lynn frowned at him. "Don't get so carried away."

"Dey be somethin' wrong with dat boy," Kiyana said.

"You've no idea," Lynn said, shaking her head.

"You said that they look like rat eyes?" Dee asked.

"Yes. They *look* like they might be rodents, but I've never caught one in a trap and none of the baits have been eaten or even touched," she said. "But, in our folklore, there be things far more worrisome."

Marty and Dee exchanged glances. Dee whispered, "Rats would be too smart for traps. Well, at least these seem to be."

"Before Adam shakes his fist of excitement again and accidentally knocks himself out—" Marty said.

Adam frowned. "Hey!"

"You almost did that in gym class once. Remember?" Marty grinned.

Adam shook his head. "Yeah, don't remind me."

Marty said, "The footprints under the pie case lead in the opposite direction of where the vent is. Is there another vent or opening on this side of your shop?"

Kiyana motioned them to come behind the pie case. "De only other place is the garbage chute. Dat's it, other than de main doors. And like I said, no one has opened them and no one except me has de keys to unlock them."

The Mystery Solvers followed Kiyana to the rear door where she received her weekly truck deliveries for her ingredients and supplies. About six or seven feet away from the door was a large metal flap that covered a four foot by four foot opening. Fresh pie crumbs and moist, gooey filling were smeared and slightly hardened on the wall and floor.

Dee said, "I'm pretty sure this is how they're getting the pies outside."

"That looks like it was recent," Marty said.

"It has ta be," Kiyana said. "I didn't leave the mess. But, I find it like this 'bout every day, even though I mopped the night before."

"And you never made the connection?" Dee asked.

"Hun, I'm so exhausted by the end of each day, I question whether I managed to clean everything thoroughly or not," Kiyana said. "And not knowing what's watching behind the vent cover, I don't like the idea of being in here after sunset."

Dee smiled. "Totally understandable. If you could do us a favor and allow us to exit this door, we'll see if we can find these—"

"Pie-Rats!" Adam said.

Dee, Marty, and Lynn glared at him. Adam blushed.

Kiyana burst into laughter. "I know it shouldn't be funny, not with all the stolen pies over the last few weeks, but dat's a good one. I definitely needed a good laugh."

Adam grinned triumphantly.

"Don't stroke his ego too much," Lynn said. "Or, you'll make him even worse."

Still laughing, Kiyana unlocked the metal door and pulled it inward. "Good luck, and thank you. Again, forgive me for my outburst earlier. You were only trying to help me, and I appreciate dat. I only hope whoever or *whatever* you find, isn't dangerous."

"Don't mention it," Dee said with a broad smile. Not only was she excited to find these rats, she felt great relief in knowing Kiyana held some trust in the Mystery Solvers and so Dee would work even harder to find the culprits, be it rats or whatever. If it were rats, she figured it was safer than other types of creatures they'd encountered before. But, she didn't realize how difficult their encounter with these thieves would be.

CHAPTER
TEN

The alleyway was different than the one on the other side of the pie shop where the ladder attached to the wall. This alley was lined with dumpsters from other businesses and somewhat darker. Even beneath the shade of the buildings the heat hung heavily. The stench of the garbage caused them to gag. They waved away buzzing flies as they walked past the dumpsters.

Dee coughed and pinched her nose. "The stench is staggering."

"Papaw would say, 'It's enough to stifle a dead cat,'" Marty said.

"No kidding," Lynn said. Her pale complexion held a greenish hue.

Marty crouched beside the dumpster outside Kiyana's door where the chute opened. He pointed. "Definitely pieces of pie under the dumpster. Probably half of a pie wasted here. Looks like their trail goes toward the waterfront."

"That's a long way to carry pies," Adam said.

"If it's rats," Dee said, "it'd have to be more than one or two."

"To tote nearly three pies?" Marty nodded. "Yes. Those pies would be heavy."

"Two and a half," Dee said.

"Still quite heavy," Lynn said.

Dee stood on tiptoe and tried to look into the dumpster under the garbage chute. She gripped the side of the greasy dumpster and grimaced. "Eww. If they dropped the pies through the chute, you'd think the pies would splatter down the inside of the dumpster, but there's little evidence of that."

She released the side of the dumpster and wiped her hands on the brick wall, which did little to get the slick grease and grime off her fingers.

Marty peered into the dumpster. "You're right. But, there's no empty pie tins, either. They'd have had to gotten them out somehow."

"How about this side door?" Adam asked. He slid the metal door to the side. "Sometimes, when you're short like me, people use these side doors to throw garbage in before the dumpster is too full. There are a few smudges of pie against the bottom, but nothing on the ground. What do you think, Lynn?"

"I think the smell and this heat are too much for me," Lynn replied. "I can't stomach getting any closer. And the flies—"

Dee thought it was cute how Adam struggled to get Lynn's approval. The two always bickered like siblings constantly teasing one another, due more to jealousy or attention-seeking, rather than actual rivals. Since they'd agreed to a name-calling truce, because it annoyed Marty and Dee, Adam and Lynn still seemed reluctant to fully lay their verbal swords down.

Dee and Marty looked around the small door Adam had opened.

Marty knelt. "Hmm. Looks like some tire marks."

"Tires?" Dee's brow rose.

He nodded. "Not big tires though. More like a small wagon or cart."

"Ahh," Dee said. "If they could move pies with a wagon, one or two rats could pull this off."

"Not too quickly, though," Marty said.

Lynn leveled an even stare at them. "Really? I'm beginning to agree with Kiyana about rats being capable of pulling something like this off in the first place."

"Rats are intelligent," Adam said.

"Perhaps for mazes," Lynn said, "but to successfully steal pies on a daily basis without leaving too much evidence? That's stretching their abilities, don't you think?"

"They can't be normal rats," Dee said.

Lynn crossed her arms. "Obviously."

"We won't know unless we investigate," Dee said.

"We're probably wasting our time," Lynn said.

Marty offered a gentle smile. "Maybe, but their trail leads toward the waterfront. If we find nothing, we'll at least be near the beach and can spend some time there before we head back to the pier with the portal."

Lynn sighed. "Fine."

"Don't forget," Dee said, "if we solve this, Kiyana will give us free pie."

Lynn twirled a finger in the air. "Yippee."

"Why so glum?" Dee asked.

"We never have fun when we get to a wonderful new place to explore," she replied. "It *always* turns into a mystery hunt. We're in Jamaica for crying out loud. Jamaica! When will we *ever* get a chance to be here again?"

"Mystery solving is fun," Dee said.

"For you," Lynn said.

Her comment cut into Dee's heart. "I thought you had fun, too."

"Yeah," Adam said.

"Usually, I do," Lynn said. "But, look at all we're missing since we have limited time. We could be on the beach and wading in the sea. Clear water. White sand. Sheesh. We're hunting for rat thieves or *Pie-Rats* instead."

"While that's true, think about it like this," Dee said. "We're helping a kind lady save her shop. Sometimes we sacrifice our wants to help others who need it."

42

Lynn sighed and nodded, but the sadness and building agitation in her eyes didn't fade.

Marty took her hand gently and smiled. "We'll hurry. Who knows? You might find another conch shell. Remember the last one you found?"

Marty's hand tightened around Lynn's. She smiled.

"The only one I've ever found," she said.

Dee smiled. Lynn finding the first shell was when she and Marty revealed their crush for one another to be known. It was also near the antique bottle they found with the treasure map inside.

"You'll find more and better things," Dee said. "I'm certain."

Lynn looked into Marty's eyes, blushed, and said, "I already have."

Dee's eyes heated with tears of joy and fought not to squeal like the teenage girl she was.

Focus. Focus. Pie-Rats.

She could rejoice about romantic things later.

CHAPTER
ELEVEN

Marty thought it odd that the thieves stealing the pies needed a wagon or a cart to haul their stolen goods away. Three pies? It was obvious humans wouldn't need a wagon or cart to transport pies. This was why he couldn't discount the notion that rats were the guilty culprits and were the most likely suspects.

The Mystery Solvers had already encountered aliens, various magical creatures only thought to exist in fairy tales, and paranormal creatures before and after the UFO crashed near their grandfather's pasture and opened the magical portal.

Rats often sought food left in dumpsters by restaurants and stores, but rats picking padlocks to steal fresh pies was unheard of. If the tiny boot was part of the rats' wardrobe, Marty would be even more stunned.

How could rodents do all these things without someone never noticing and reporting them?

Other than the Mystery Solvers, the alleyway was vacant, so no one would interfere with their search for clues. He imagined at night this alley would be too dark for anyone to dare venture through it.

The alley was creepy enough during the day for him to even entertain the idea of surveilling the activities after sunset. Of course, it was like any other mystery. Being in an unfamiliar place and searching for an unknown thief caused him to question any unusual sound and wonder what had made the noise.

Marty kept a watchful eye while slowly walking past each dumpster. Occasionally, he'd peer into an open dumpster but noticed nothing of interest. Most of the dumpsters had been emptied recently but the remnants of rotting food scraps were stuck to the bottom and the dumpsters' inner walls, which attracted fly swarms during the sweltering summer heat.

Dee followed behind Marty. She stooped and looked behind and under the dumpsters while Lynn walked beside Marty with her arms crossed. Adam focused more on the small ladders that led to the rooftops.

"What are you looking for, Adam?" Marty asked.

He shrugged. "The Pie-Rats might be keeping watch."

"During the day?" Dee said.

"Why not? They have to know someone will eventually figure out what they're doing," Adam said.

Lynn giggled.

"What?" Adam asked.

"Nothing," she said, playfully waving her hand. "It's just you've gotten so much better at looking for rational clues."

"Uh, thanks," Adam said, blushing slightly and an odd smile curled his lips. An unexpected compliment was never a bad thing and had caught Adam off guard.

"Ah, don't let it go over your head," Lynn said.

Adam eyed her with a shrewd stare. "Hey! Is our truce over?"

"By no means," Lynn replied. "I meant 'to' your head, not *over*."

He frowned while searching her eyes. "Su-u-re, you did."

"Honest," Lynn said. "Not teasing you like you did me is a hard habit for me to break, too."

"So you admit it, then?"

"Admit what?"

Adam adjusted his cap. A smug expression formed on his face. "You enjoyed our snide remarks toward one another."

She shrugged slightly. "At times. But I also have to admit, you were going far too overboard with it."

Adam smiled. "Agreed. Sorry about that."

"It's all in the past. Just because I confessed that, doesn't mean I want to resume."

"Yeah, sure, I understand."

Halfway down the alley, one of the wheels of whatever had transported the pies had rolled through some sticky sauce, which darkened the tire's tread marks for several feet. The alley slanted downward and the afternoon sunlight brightened. In the distance, the bright blue water shimmered with intensity. Children and adults were walking the beach. Several small boats coasted through the shallow surf.

"Come on," Marty said, pointing at the greasy tire marks. "Looks like the wagon or cart probably picked up speed and headed to the water."

The Mystery Solvers hurried down the alley and shielded their eyes with the backs of their hands as they stepped into the full force of the sunlight. After their eyes adjusted, Marty half sprinted across the white sand following the wheels' trenches until they ended at the sea.

"That's impossible," Adam said.

"What?" Dee asked.

"The wagon or cart went into the water? The pies and the wagon would've sank, right?"

Marty sighed. "Not necessarily."

"What?" Adam asked. "Any wagon should sink."

"A metal wagon would definitely sink. But not if it's made primarily of plastic," Marty said. "And, if the wheels are plastic and hollow, they might have enough buoyancy to stay afloat. At least for a little while."

Lynn put her hand against her brow like she was saluting, but she was preventing the sun from hampering her view. She seemed to be studying the water. With her dark makeup streaks down her pale cheeks, she almost looked like a ghoul. "The tide here is minimal, so no current should drag a small raft outward. They'd have to paddle."

Dee nodded. "Good observation, but which way?"

"That's a guessing game," Marty said.

"We should split up," Adam said.

Marty shook his head. "No. We're not familiar with the area and if any of us got lost, we'd be hard pressed to find each other before we returned to the portal."

Dee grinned. "Then what do you suggest, big brother?"

"About a hundred yards in that direction is the pier we came out from under," he replied.

"You think they'd go there?" Lynn asked. "Or are you wanting us to use the portal to go home?"

Marty shook his head. "Oh, I don't plan for us to go home just yet. But, oddly enough, we might've walked right past them when we came out of the portal."

Dee frowned and her neck stiffened. "What?"

"Let's hurry to the pier and I'll show you," Marty said.

CHAPTER
TWELVE

As the Mystery Solvers came closer to the pier, a male teenager that appeared to be about their age—if Dee were to guess—was pulling a blue plastic wagon out of the water. The wagon was stamped with the '**PROPERTY OF**' sticker from one of the local hotels.

The dark-skinned teen with thick, curly hair, heaved the wagon from the water and tugged it through the wet sand where the tires mired down. He wore olive-green cargo shorts and a light green polo shirt with the same hotel's logo above the shirt's pocket as on the wagon sticker. His name tag indicated his name was Tarone.

Dee approached him. "Excuse me, Tarone."

Tarone turned the wagon upright to empty the rest of the sea water. "Yes?"

"Who'd push a hotel wagon into the sea?" she asked.

"No idea," he replied. He frowned while tilting the wagon us and grunted. "But it happens more and more lately."

"Really?" Dee asked.

Tarone nodded.

"Why don't you lock the wagons up?" Adam said.

Tarone grinned. "We do. We use chains and padlocks to secure them, but almost every day we or one of de other hotels have to retrieve a wagon from the sea."

"Interesting," Dee said.

"How so?" Tarone asked with a curious frown.

"Oh." Dee shrugged. "That seems a lot of trouble for someone to pick a lock only to throw a wagon into the water."

"Perhaps," he said. "But, I guess someone uses them for something. The tire marks go a long ways up the beach."

Dee looked at Marty. "There has to be some kind of pattern."

Marty nodded.

Tarone said, "There is, actually."

"Oh?" Dee said.

"Yes," Tarone said, "the wagon seems to be taken before the tide goes out. It floats for a while and always ends up near the pier, except today. At least I didn't have to walk dat far."

"Hmm," Dee said.

"What other security methods does your hotel have?" Marty asked.

Tarone shrugged and set the wagon's wheels atop drier sand. "We have night security officers, but they never seem able to catch anyone taking a wagon. Whoever steals them ... they seem invisible or incredibly fast."

"Thanks," Dee said.

Tarone grinned. "Now, if you'll pardon me, I've got to get this back to the hotel."

Dee nodded.

She waited until Tarone was gone before she grinned at Marty.

"What?" Marty said.

"Invisible?" Dee said.

Marty shook his head. "No. We know this *isn't* a ghost."

"Do we?" she said.

Lynn rolled her eyes. "Of course we know, Dee. Goodness. Ordinary ghosts cannot move physical objects. I don't know why you'd even hint that. Ghosts would have no need to eat pie. They *don't* eat."

"Besides," Adam said. "We found the boot of a Pie-Rat and plenty of other evidence."

Dee laughed softly and waved a playful hand. "I know. Just teasing. It *is* interesting that the wagons disappear at the same time each night and get stuck as the tide goes out."

A seagull shriek farther down the beach near the pier. A silvery shimmer caught Dee's eye. "Look."

"That's a pie pan," Marty said.

Adam pointed at some small prints in the dry sand. "Those have to be rat tracks."

"Maybe," Lynn said. "Or some sort of rodent. They don't belong to birds."

"Whatever they are, there seems to be a lot of them," Dee said.

"Unless they backtracked or haven't been erased for several days," Marty said.

"That's true," Dee said. "The tide doesn't seem to rise too high here. Come on. Let's see what's in the pan the seagull's picking at."

THIRTEEN

M arty shooed the bird off, and Dee picked up the flimsy, aluminum pan.

"It's starting to make better sense," Marty said.

"How's that?" Adam asked.

"When we first came through the portal, I kept stepping on thin metal items, remember? In the dark, I couldn't tell what they were. That's what I wanted us to check for. Maybe I was stepping on pie pans?"

Lynn cringed. "You mean we might've walked right past a mischief?"

"It's possible," Marty said.

Adam frowned. "What's a mischief?"

Dee said, "That's what a group of rats is called."

"Fitting," Lynn said, "if it's rats stealing the pies."

Marty laughed. "That's definitely mischief."

"At least they have good taste," Adam said.

"We don't know that yet," Lynn said with a wry grin. "No one's given us any pie."

Dee looked at the pie tin. Bits of crust and fruit were stuck to the bottom.

Adam gagged. "I don't think I want to test taste *that*."

"None of us do," Dee said. "But we're closer to solving these thefts than anyone else has been."

In the shadows under the pier several small creatures scurried. If they were rats, they appeared to be running upright instead of on all fours. They were much larger than regular rats, too.

"Hurry," Marty said, pointing. "I think I see them."

"Careful," Adam said. "They might attack us."

"I bet with little cutlasses and daggers, huh?" Lynn asked.

"No. But wild rats are known to bite and carry disease," Adam said. "And since we don't know the area, the last thing we want is to be bitten by an infectious rat and trying to get medical attention."

Lynn scoffed. "What's happened to you?"

Adam looked confused. "What do you mean?"

"You're more deductive and," Lynn said, "erm, how do I say this without being offensive? You're much smarter than normal."

"I own a hamster and have had a couple of rats for pets," Adam said, and he didn't seem offended by her covert, snide remark.

"Eww," Lynn said, scrunching her nose. "Really? Rats for pets?"

"Sure. The ones I had were cleaner and more well-behaved than some cats," Adam said. "They're social animals."

"So why would these attack us?" Dee asked.

"Well," Adam said. "They're already known thieves, can pick locks, and steal wagons and pies without conscience. Biting us wouldn't be unexpected. They've got a good thing going. I'm sure they don't want to lose that."

Marty chuckled. "He's got you there."

The rat silhouettes vanished into the darker crevices beneath the pier by the time the Mystery Solvers reached the bridge. Perhaps due to the magical portal where they'd wound up in Jamaica was what made the area under the bridge seem darker. The harsh sunlight was suddenly dulled.

"Are you sure you saw rats?" Dee asked.

Marty nodded. "No mistake about it."

Adam searched the rocks with fearful eyes. He stood with one foot still in the sunlight and was more reluctant than the others about stepping completely under the darkened pier.

"We're not confronting a vampire, Adam," Lynn said.

Adam shrugged. "We don't know *what* we might actually encounter."

"He's right, so be careful," Marty said.

"I don't see any rats," Dee said. "Any of you have your flashlight handy?"

A small flashlight flicked on, but it didn't belong to any of the Mystery Solvers. Four sets of crimson eyes glowed from the stacked, broken rocks. The light from the flashlight illuminated the four rats dressed in small clothes. The rat in front of the other three had white fur. Its face and limbs glowed in a ghostly fashion, making him more visible.

"I see them," Lynn said.

"U-u-uh," Adam stuttered. "M-m-me, too."

"Avast, ye mateys," the white rat said with a shrill voice. He slashed the air with his tiny cutlass. "What brings ya to our lair?"

CHAPTER

FOURTEEN

"Lair?" Dee said. "You're under a *pier*. Not much of a lair."

"It'll do," the white rat said. "What'd you expect anyway? A troll? Trolls don't complain about their housing. At least, not *here*."

The other three rats laughed in high-pitched voices.

"Good one, Pierre," a black rat, wearing a cavalier hat, said.

"Thanks, Jules," Pierre said with a haughty expression on his furry face.

"T-trolls?" Adam asked nervously.

Lynn frowned. "He was joking."

"But with the portal," Adam said, "it's possible."

"That's only if the portal's still there," Marty said.

"Oh, it's here," Pierre said, stepping out where he was better seen. He held a small cutlass in his right paw, a tiny dagger in his left, wore a tricorn hat, and a leather vest. His short leggings stopped above his bushy knees, and he wore black boots like the one wedged in the ceiling tile. "But, if you're aiming to go back through the portal, it's going to cost ya."

"Oh?" Dee said. "Why?"

Pierre shrugged his tiny shoulders. "Troll bridges have tolls, so do we."

"We didn't pay anything when we came through," Lynn said angrily.

"Oooh," Pierre said. "Then ya'll have to pay double to go back through. Toss your packs to us. And don't make any sudden moves."

"And if we refuse?" Dee said.

The other three rats stepped out with their tiny blades drawn. They wore variant types of pirate garb. The striped rat wore a tattered scarf over his head and around his neck. Its little rat ears protruded through slits in the scarf. The gray rat had a patch over his right eye and a tricorn hat with a skull and crossbones emblem.

The mini flashlight glowed behind them on the rock where they had set it. Had they been in an enclosed dark room without the faintest sliver of sunlight, the flashlight beam might've cast large shadows of the rats on an opposing wall. But with the side of the bridge open, the light lacked any intimidating effect, if they'd have hoped to project one.

"Then, ya'll be at our mercy, Lassie," Pierre said.

Dee made fists and rested them on her hips in a near Supergirl pose. She offered her best hardened frown and narrowed her eyes. "I don't think you've thought this through."

The rats slashed their metal cutlasses through the air, almost mimicking movie musketeers.

Lynn shook her head. "Are you trying to kill gnats with those blades or what?"

Without much success, Pierre deepened his voice. "Come closer, and we'll show you how sharp our blades are."

Unfortunately, Adam was the only Mystery Solver intimidated by their attitudes. "Exactly *what* do you want us to pay?"

"What have ye?" Jules asked. He lifted his eyepatch for several moments, squinting to see. It was obvious the patch was decorative and unnecessary. He quickly positioned it over his eye again.

Lynn shook her head. "Great. We're getting held up by rat fiends."

"Pirates, Lass, pirates," the gray-striped rat said. This rat wore a lady buccaneer hat. "We take what we need when we need it."

"You heard Eloise," Pierre said. "So, hand over your loot."

"We have no *loot*," Dee said.

Pierre frowned. "Ya have packs! That's loot!"

Eloise leapt from the rock and slashed her cutlass through the air as she landed. Her frilly hat was caught by a slight breeze and almost dislodged the hat. Perhaps fearful she'd lose the hat, she grabbed it and lost her footing. If not for her long tail wrapping around a piece of driftwood, she'd have fallen face first. She chattered, despite her slight embarrassment, and cleared her throat. "That's for us to decide. Drop your packs on the ground. Or else, face our wrath!"

"Sorry," Marty said. "We have no pie to offer."

"Pie?" Jules said, scrunching his nose. "We have *lots* of pie."

"Pie-Rats," Adam half whispered. "I told you guys! Right, Lynn?"

The rats turned their attention to Adam.

Lynn shook her head. "Sadly, you were right about their weapons and clothing."

"You dare mock us?" Pierre said, glaring at Adam. He showed his yellowed teeth and hissed. "Best you run away, young lad, as it seems you're ready to. Ya not even brave enough to set foot under the pier. Run! Be prepared to be chased by Chase when you do. He's lightning fast and can jab your ankles with his blade before you escape. If you're lucky, he won't sever your Achilles heel and cripple you."

The gray rat eyed Adam with a fierce glare and grinned menacingly. The rat's eyes narrowed and he flashed his teeth. "I'm Chase. Ready for a fast sprint?"

Adam shook his head and took a step backward. "Um, n-o-o-t particularly."

Pierre slashed his cutlass in the air and said, "Then step into the shadows, lad. *If* you dare."

Lynn rolled her eyes and stared at Dee. "This is *so* ... unbelievable."

"Did you come through the portal?" Marty asked.

"Of course," Pierre said. "The rats here are far too primitive. I'd think you'd have assumed that. We've yet to find any rats that speak or understand us. Unless, *you* know of any? If so, tell us where, perhaps they'll join us in our endeavors."

"So the rats can speak where you're from?" Dee asked.

Pierre gave her a shrewd stare. "Obviously."

Adam stared past the rats toward the darker recesses under the bridge. "You came through the same portal as we did?"

"Aye, matey," Jules said. "Some time ago."

"And you never left?" Dee said.

"Why should we?" Pierre said. "We have more than we ever had in our realm."

"You mean from stealing?" Dee said.

"That's what pirates do," Eloise said, offering a slight curtsy. "Correct?"

"Were you pirates before you came to our world?" Adam asked.

"No," Pierre said.

Lynn laughed.

Pierre frowned and sized her up. "What's so funny?"

"Pirates are so ... two centuries ago," she replied.

Pierre's brow crumpled with confusion. "So?"

"You're in the *wrong* century!" she said.

Eloise hissed. "I beg to differ. Seems pirates are quite honored on this isle."

"Honored?" Marty said. "What brought you to that conclusion?"

Pierre frowned. "Aren't they?"

"No," Dee said. "Thieves are never honored."

"You sure?" Pierre asked with genuine curiosity. "'Cause everywhere we look, humans pay good money to dress in this fancy garb. Of course, *much* larger than what we wear. No matter. Just do as we say. Drop the bags and hand over the loot. Or *else*."

In a defiant tone, Lynn said, "Or else, *what?*"

"You'll be walking de plank," Pierre said.

Jules whispered, "We don't *have* a plank."

"Oh, yeah," Pierre said, frustrated and disappointed. He scratched his furry chin for several moments. "You'll have to walk off the pier then!"

"Like that's going to happen," Dee said, taking a step closer. Lynn stepped beside her.

Seeming unsure of himself, Pierre's nervous gaze went from each of the Mystery Solvers and finally met Marty's eyes.

Marty stepped between the rats and the other three Mystery Solvers. "Even with your tiny weapons, you must realize you're no match for me, much less against the four of us."

Pierre took a deep breath and expelled it. "I'm ready to meet your challenge."

Pierre's three rat companions stood their ground alongside him, but they were more apprehensive and their expressions were conflicted. They kept looking over their shoulders toward the rocks where their flashlight glowed. Dee expected them to retreat and let Pierre face Marty alone.

"I don't want to harm any of you," Marty said. "Dressed like you are, you're too cute to punt through the air like a football."

Pierre glared. "*Cute?*"

"Punt?" Chase asked, taking a few steps backwards.

Dee snickered. "Where'd you rats get those dainty pirate clothes anyway?"

Pierre's eyes shifted side-to-side and he looked down, examining his clothes.

"Someone named, 'Ken'," Eloise said.

Jules grinned and straightened the front of his vest. He whispered, "Sparrow's the name of the chap I took mine from. He's in several documentaries."

Lynn frowned. "Wait. Is that how you learned about pirates?"

Eloise nodded. "Yes. Adventurous documentaries and we *love* adventure."

Lynn shook her head. "No less than Dee loves solving mysteries, but I hate to disappoint you, those films *aren't* documentaries. They're fiction. Made up tales."

Eloise and Jules exchanged shocked expressions.

"They're not real accounts?" Eloise asked.

"No," Marty said with a grin.

"Lies," Pierre said. "What I saw couldn't have been made up."

Dee giggled. "Why would we lie about that?"

"Look here!" Pierre said. He sheathed his blade. "We're getting off course, and we've yet to board a seafaring vessel. You entered our lair so you *must* pay a toll or else."

Marty slid his backpack off his shoulders and set it on the compacted sand. As he unzipped the pack, Pierre rubbed his fuzzy forepaws together.

"Yes!" Pierre grinned. "That's more like it."

Marty rummaged through the bag's contents.

Pierre whispered to the other rats. "Maybe he has some honey roasted peanuts or something salty."

"Please something salty," Jules said. "I'm getting sick of pie."

In a glum voice, Marty said, "We really don't carry a lot of valuables when we go through the portal. Basically, changes of clothes are what we take. Depending upon what the temperature is in the place we arrive. We'd freeze to death if we came to a snowy place dressed like we are now. So, we have nothing you'd value because, well, you're much smaller than we are, so our clothing is of no use to you."

Jules stood on his hind tiptoes, straining to see what was in the bag, but from a distance. "Let us discern what's of value."

"I do have one item," Marty said. "It should really surprise you."

The rats remained out of Marty's reach, but leaned closer with curiosity. Their widened eyes watched in awe and anticipation.

In a swift movement, Marty raised his high-beamed LED flashlight and clicked it on. He aimed for their eyes.

"Arrgh!" Pierre squealed in pain and then wailed, "I'm blind!"

The other rats dropped their tiny cutlasses and scurried in circles on their hind legs while covering their eyes. They bumped into one another. Jules tripped, causing Eloise to lose her balance and smack into a rock. Pierre squalled and rubbed his eyes, while fumbling to pull his cutlass. Once he unsheathed it, it was knocked to the ground by Chase who accidentally rammed into Pierre's back.

"Drat!" Pierre said, dropping on all fours and patting the ground.

Adam hurried and scooped up several of their weapons and stuck them in his cargo shorts pocket before the rats fully regained their sight. He then reached for Jules' blade, but the rat ripped his eye patch off.

Jules sneered, grabbed his cutlass, and said, "You forgot I was wearing a patch, didn't you? I can see you."

Marty aimed the flashlight at Jules and its blaring light struck the rat's unpatched eye.

Jules moaned and dropped the cutlass. He raised his forelimbs in surrender. "Why? Why'd you do that?"

Eloise patted the ground. "Pierre, why do you always get us into trouble? What do we do now?"

"Beg for mercy?" Pierre whimpered. "Parley! Parley!"

"You think that's actually going to work?" Eloise asked.

"It did for Sparrow."

"You're *not* Sparrow," she quipped.

"I've a better idea," Marty said.

CHAPTER

FIFTEEN

E ach of the Mystery Solvers grabbed a rat by the tail and
hefted them off the compacted sand and kept them at arms'
length.

Dee said, "Are you guys going to calm yourselves?"

"Hey!" Pierre said. "Hands off! Put me down!"

"You heard 'em," Jules said. "Put us down."

Fuming, Pierre said, "You really crossed a line grabbing us like
this, matey. So unfair."

Adam cautiously held Chase out away from himself. "Don't
bite us."

Pierre made a soured expression. "That's be undignified, now
wouldn't it? Thinks of the germs we'd get. Phht. But, you'd deserve it
since grabbing us is even more undignified."

"Bite a human? Eww. That's rather gross," Eloise said, "if you ask
me. Now, if you won't unhand us, at least don't hold us by the tails.
You might injure us."

"Oh," Dee said. "You'd worry about your injuries and your
welfare, but you threatened to stab us if we refused to give you our
valuables?"

"That was Pierre's doing," Chase said. "He's always had a big mouth and tends to think being loud and making threats will intimidate humans into giving us what we want."

Adam held Chase up and gave the rat a stern look. "You were quite convincing yourself when you said you'd chase me down and stab my ankles. But now that the table has turned—"

Chase offered a sheepish grin and made a pleading gesture with his forepaws. "For what it's worth, I'm sorry about that. Truly sorry. Besides, had you run, I'd have never caught you. I mean, think about the reality of that. Your stride's far greater than any rat. Even at my fastest, I'd never get near you."

Adam gently grabbed the scruff of Chase's neck and released the rat's tail. "This is a better way to handle them. Eloise is right. Holding them by the tails can injure them."

Chase frowned and crossed his forearms. "You knew this all along?"

Adam nodded. "Of course. I had a couple of rats for pets before."

The rats looked bewildered.

Pierre blinked and stared at Adam. "You fiend."

"Fiend?" Adam said.

Lynn laughed.

Pierre said, "Are rats so inferior in your world that they've no pride in allowing themselves to be pets."

"Rats are social animals," Dee said.

"Social?" Pierre said.

Eloise huffed. "*Animals*? You consider us subpar and degrade our kind by keeping us as pets? We're far more superior to the rats in your realm."

"Scientifically," Marty said, "we consider ourselves as part of the animal kingdom."

"And rightly so!" Pierre said. "Yet, you take pride in keeping us locked in cages."

"I've never harmed any of my pets," Adam said. "I kept the cage cleaned, made sure they have fresh food and water at all times, and even taught them tricks."

"Oh," Jules said, "that's *so-o-o* much better. Make us your circus property."

"I did no such thing," Adam said. "They had better lives than staying in the pet store. It could've been worse had they been in a biology lab where scientists do ex—"

Marty shook his head. "Let's not go there."

"Wait," Pierre said. "What do these scientists do? Tell us."

Marty explained the various types of experiments scientists have done by using rats for scientific discovery in drug tests, cancer tests, and other mental tests.

"And *you're* afraid of *us*?" Eloise asked.

"Afraid?" Dee said. "No, just cautious. No one likes to be bitten."

"For fear of being captured and caged," Pierre said, "I can see why the rats in this realm bite and claw. We're not like that."

"Says the rat who threatened to stab us," Lynn said.

"Do we really look like that big a threat?" Pierre asked.

"Minus the weapons, you're too adorable to be vicious," Dee said. "But you are thieves, and you're making a wonderful pie shop owner miserable."

"So we took a few pies?" Jules said. "What's the harm in that?"

"You are affecting her livelihood," Dee said.

Eloise's voice saddened. "Really? We never considered that."

Dee nodded. "And why did you need so many pies for the four of you?"

"For the lesser rats," Pierre said, nobly. "They don't understand us, but they have befriended us because we feed them."

"Look," Marty said. "If we set you down, will you promise not to attack?"

"We weren't really going to attack," Pierre said, glumly. "We wanted your respect and I suppose that by making you fear us, you'd show enough respect not to capture us and you'd leave us alone. But, seeing as you captured us *anyways*—"

"Just answer the question," Eloise said. "I promise I won't bite you and since you've taken our weapons, you have little to worry about from those now."

"Yes," Pierre said. "I won't bite you, either. The thought of getting human skin caught between my teeth."

Jules and Chase both nodded.

"Promise you won't run away?" Dee said. "We mean you no harm and would really like to know more about you and the realm where you've come from."

"Sure," Chase said. "I'd feel safer being on the ground. Although this height isn't too dizzying, there's always the chance of being dropped. We certainly won't run through the portal. We can't. The dangers of returning to our homes on the other side of the portal is far worse than even what your scientists could do to us."

"Okay," Marty said. "Truce. We're setting you down."

After the Mystery Solvers released the rats, the rats stood and straightened their attire. Adam handed Pierre his pirate hat. After Pierre adjusted it, he groomed his face with his paws and the other rats did the same.

"What dangers prevent you from returning home?" Dee asked.

"Cats," Pierre said.

"We have cats," Lynn said.

"Talking cats? Cats with stun guns?" Eloise asked. "Mini tanks?"

Lynn cocked a brow and shook her head. The grin tugging at the edges of her lips indicated she was seconds from bursting into laughter. Dee had seen that expression far too often and figured Lynn thought the rats were pulling their legs. "Your cats talk and use weapons?"

"Tanks, really?" Adam said in disbelief.

Pierre said, "You'd expect any less, given you've heard us talk, and we have weapons? Of course, ours aren't as advanced as the cats. And cats are the dominant species in our world. They are, as I've heard others say here, 'top dog'. Only, we have no dogs to keep the cats in check. The imbalance isn't right, and if only your animals spoke, we might've had a chance to recruit a pack of dogs to terrorize the cats."

Adam eased the cutlasses from his shorts pocket and examined them. "Wow. These *are* metal."

"Of course they're metal," Pierre said. "We brought them through the portal with us. By accident, though."

"Careful with those," Chase said. "You could get a nasty cut from them."

"I thought they were hard plastic," Dee said.

Adam shook his head and handed a cutlass to her. "Nope. See for yourselves."

Dee took one blade and gently rubbed her finger across the edge. "Yeesh. Your false threats are now more concerning."

"We weren't going to actually harm you," Pierre said. "I swear. We just wanted you to leave us alone."

"We never intended to harm you, either," Dee said. "We were just trying to get to the bottom of our investigation and figure out who was stealing the pies."

"And the clues led to us?" Eloise asked.

"Yes."

"How?" Pierre asked. He hammered a fist atop his other forepaws. "We covered our tracks perfectly."

Dee laughed. "You actually left a *lot* of tracks to follow."

Dee explained the messy pie case and the small boot prints under the case, and then Adam talked about the little boot they'd found wedged in the ceiling tile. Marty told them about the vent cover having no screws and pie filling smudges on the vent.

Eloise eyed Chase and shook her head with disappointment. "So that's where you lost the boot? I told you not to take the small piece of pie with you."

Chase shrugged. "I was hungry. Climbing and running as quickly as I do, expends a lot of energy. Of course, if all we keep eating is pie, I'm going to become too fat to run, like Jules."

Jules scrunched his nose. "Hey!"

Dee extended her hand toward the four rats and the rats warily leaned back. "So now we understand each others' motives. Truce?"

The four rats exchanged glances with one another, nodded, and did fist bumps with Dee and then with the other three Mystery Solvers.

SIXTEEN

The rats sheathed their tiny blades and seemed more at ease. The heat of the afternoon's sea breeze flowed beneath the pier, sea birds made sharp sounds as they flew, and a large brown pelican landed promptly under the pier and waddled toward them. The rats ran and stumbled in their attempt to hide in the safety of the rocks.

Dee shooed the large pelican. It turned, waddled away, and reluctantly flew away. "It's safe now."

The rats peered out from the rock crevices and sniffed the air. Confident the pelican was gone, they returned to where the Mystery Solvers stood.

"Thanks," Pierre said. "That beast almost caught and swallowed Jules the other day."

"I didn't see it," Jules said.

"Because of that stupid patch you insist on wearing," Eloise said. "You didn't see the bird because it approached from your blindside. That patch will get you killed yet."

"But it's, as they say, 'Cool!'," he replied.

"Oh, well, being dead is not cool, other than your stiffened corpse turning cold," Eloise said. "Since the four of us are all that we'll know of our kind, we cannot afford to lose any of our group."

"What do you mean?" Dee asked.

"Our portal is gone," Eloise replied.

"Wait," Marty said. "You said that you came through the portal by accident, right?"

Pierre nodded.

"How?" Dee asked.

"You do *know* what '*accident*' means, right?" Pierre said.

"Of course," Dee said. "But if not on purpose, something caused you to bumble your way through the portal."

"We were hiding on a side street when a mini tank operator noticed us," Pierre said. "We darted into a dark alleyway and didn't realize an actual portal was at the end of the alley. We ran through it, thinking it was a shadow."

"Why didn't the tank come after you?" Adam asked.

Jules adjusted his eyepatch and said, "They fired and caused an explosion. A wall crashed on top of the portal. At least that's what we *think* happened. We didn't actually see the outcome."

Pierre nodded. "So, even if we wanted to go home, we can't. Not through the portal you came through. Yours is a different portal. Ours is no longer accessible."

Adam frowned. "That makes no sense."

"What?" Pierre and Dee asked at the same time.

"How can the same portal connect to two different realms or worlds or whatever you call them, at the same time?"

Marty shrugged. "We're still trying to figure out how portals work. Perhaps our two portals overlapped and after the cat tank blew up the rats' portal, ours appeared in place of it?"

"If true, that's concerning," Dee said.

"Why?" Lynn asked.

"If a portal could be destroyed without our knowledge and another replaced it, we might accidentally end up in a different world than we came from and become stuck there."

"Like us," Eloise said.

"See?" Pierre said, staring at Marty. "Accidentally."

"So you can't get home?" Marty asked.

The rats shook their heads.

"That's a shame," Dee said.

"Oh," Pierre said. "It's not *that* bad. This place is beautiful, other than that pesky, big bird."

"If you're staying here," Dee said, "you can't keep stealing from Kiyana."

Eloise nodded. "I know. I feel so terrible."

"Whether you find a way to return to your realm or not," Dee said, "you need to make restitution."

"I agree," Eloise said.

"Why?" Pierre said. "It's not like she has a shortage of pies. Every day more pies are stocked in the glass case."

"They don't appear by magic," Lynn said.

Pierre frowned. "They don't?"

"No," Dee said. "Kiyana sells the pies to customers by the slice, and that's how she pays her bills and buys the ingredients she needs to make them. But, every time you steal her pies, you're cutting into her livelihood. She said she might close her shop by the end of the month. If she does, you have no more pie."

Chase rubbed his slightly chubby stomach. "I'm getting sick of pie anyways."

"That's not the point," Dee said.

Pierre lowered his head in shame. "I—I wasn't aware—"

"Don't lie," Eloise said, resting her forepaws on her hips like a mother did when scolding a child. "I told you last week that she was crying when I watched her through the vent cover."

Pierre sighed. "I know, but I didn't think she was crying because of the missing pies."

"What *else* would she be crying about?" Lynn asked.

"Human stuff?" Pierre said.

Dee frowned. "What kind of *human* stuff?"

Pierre shrugged. "You name it."

"We need to make this right," Eloise said. "I need to."

"Me, too," Jules said.

Chase nodded. "I want to, as well."

The three rats glared at Pierre.

With a glum expression, Pierre said, "Yes. Me, too."

Dee smiled. "Good. I've an idea."

CHAPTER

SEVENTEEN

"You may not like this," Dee said. "But I think the best way to resolve this is for the four of you to talk to Kiyana."

For several seconds, it looked like the rats were washing and grooming one another's face, but they were whispering with one another. Evident fear shown in their expressions and the nervousness of their chattering.

"What?" Lynn said. "You saw how angry Kiyana got because of the absurd suggestion before."

"Yes," Dee said, waving her hand toward the four rats. "But now, she can see for herself that we were right."

Marty shook his head. "Dee, I'm not sure how she'll take this information. While seeing is believing, it's so out of the ordinary, she might think she's losing her mind."

"She's *already* losing her mind and wants to give up her business because she has no idea why or what's been stealing her pies," Dee said.

"That's true," Marty said.

Dee smiled. "Now, we have evidence."

"We'll have to wait until night to take them to her shop," Lynn said. She stared at the sea with disappointment in her eyes. "And by nightfall, it'll be too late for the beach or any other sightseeing."

Dee's smile broadened into a wide grin. "*Not* necessarily."

"What do you suggest?" Marty asked. "Should anyone see them dressed like little pirates, it will draw attention, and should they speak, they'll definitely get others' attention. I know one of them has to talk *all* the time." Marty gave a stern look at Pierre.

Eloise grinned. "You know that's right."

Dee never thought a rat could blush, but Pierre's reddening skin showed through his white fur.

Chase, Eloise, and Jules all stared at Pierre and said, "*Pierre?*"

He shrugged and stared at his feet. "Sorry."

Dee unzipped her pack. "Each of us could hide a rat in our pack."

Pierre's eyes widened. With a fierce thrust of his paw, he pointed at her backpack. "What? You expect us to be zipped inside your packs? We'll hyperventilate or die from the heat or perhaps, since we speak and look sooo *cute*, like *you* keep saying, you'll sell us to a circus or something. Especially, the boy with the backwards hat. He's already *owned* rats as pets."

"You can trust us," Dee said.

Pierre crossed his forelimbs. "Humph. I think I'd rather trust the cats."

"Seriously?" Dee said. "If we wanted to harm you, we'd could've when we had each of you by the tail."

Eloise gave Pierre a stern stare. "Pierre, you'll do like she requests. All of us will. We've taken enough of their time, and taken far more from Kiyana than we ever should have. So get inside the bag."

"Or what?" Pierre said with a frown.

"Remember the big brown bird?" Eloise asked.

"Yeah?"

"It's waddling back. See?" she pointed. The large shadow of a bird was almost under the pier and seemed to be headed in their direction.

Pierre's red, beady eyes widened. He gasped and ran to Dee's pack and threw himself headlong into the opening. "Zip it! Zip it! For the love of all that's decent and wonderful, zip it!"

Dee and Lynn burst into laughter when the long shadow turned out to be a tiny pigeon walking under the pier.

Pierre peeked from the pack's opening. He scoffed and shook his head. "Nice one, Eloise."

"Get inside and let her zip the pack," Eloise said with a sly grin. She rubbed her forepaws together.

Pierre grumbled and allowed Dee to zip her pack.

Chase hurried into Adam's pack, while Eloise chose Lynn's pack for safety, and Jules climbed inside Marty's.

CHAPTER

EIGHTEEN

When the Mystery Solvers arrived at Kiyana's Pie Shop, they waited on the street until the last customer exited, and then they entered with their packs over their shoulders.

Dee smiled at Kiyana, and Kiyana returned the smile but her eyes revealed her curiosity.

Dee slid her pack from her shoulders. With a confident smile, she said, "We have solved your mystery."

Kiyana cocked a brow. "Ah, 'ave ya, now? What did you find out?"

Dee started to set her pack on top of the glass case, but then thought about how a health inspector might view her reveal, even though the rats had frequented the pie shop countless times already.

Instead, she went to one of the two empty tables and set her pack down. Lynn and Adam did the same, but Marty was more reluctant and kept his pack on his shoulders.

Kiyana cocked her head to the side and frowned curiously as she came around from behind the counter. "What 'ave ya got there?"

"Marty?" Dee said, directing him with her head to join them at the table.

Marty sighed and placed his pack on the table.

After the Mystery Solvers unzipped and set their packs slightly on their sides, the four rats stepped out dressed in their pirate garb.

Anger caused Kiyana's upper lip to curl. She fumed. She flung her white towel onto her shoulder and rested her hands on her hips. "Oh, now dat's not funny. Why make a joke at my expense, eh? Here, I thought you had some serious evidence, something dat might give me a way to find the thief, and ya go ta a pet shop and dress up a bunch of rats like pirates."

"Pie-Rats," Adam said.

Kiyana glared. "The funniness of dat is no longer humorous. How dare you insult me like dis!"

Pierre brushed himself off and stood upright. "For someone who makes such delicious pies, you certainly have a sour attitude to these young people. We are the ones who ... stole your pies."

Eloise said, "And we're very sorry."

Pierre held his hat in his front forepaws and nodded. "So sorry."

Kiyana's mouth gaped and her brow rose. She looked like she might scream, but no sound came from her mouth. She stumbled slightly and grabbed a stool from the neighboring table to steady herself. Marty gently held her elbow in case she happened to faint. After a few seconds, he helped Kiyana sit on the stool, but she didn't speak and couldn't take her eyes off the rats. Marty moved closer to Dee.

Pierre eyed Kiyana. "These guys brought us here to make us accountable for stealing the pies and see how we can make right what we did wrong."

Eloise took off her hat and did a slight curtesy. "Pierre's not lying. These teens aren't lying, either."

The four rats stood side by side and offered slight smiles, but Pierre, obviously ashamed of having stolen, kept his gaze downward, afraid of looking Kiyana in the eyes and perhaps worried about what she would require as the proper punishment.

Marty nudged Dee and whispered, "You best say something. I

told you she wouldn't take this well, and she might still faint or go into shock."

Dee nodded and walked to Kiyana. Dee placed a gentle hand on Kiyana's shoulder. Kiyana jumped slightly. "It's okay."

"How?" Kiyana said, shaking her head. Despite being near tears, she smiled and pointed at the rats. "How's this possible? Do they have batteries or are they computerized? RC maybe? Are these real rats?"

Pierre's shame turned to slight anger at her odd line of immediate questions. "Of course, we're *real* rats."

Kiyana stiffened.

Eloise shushed Pierre and raised a paw like she was about to backhand him. Pierre cringed and moved away from Eloise to the other side of Jules.

"Sorry, Kiyana," Pierre said.

Dee squeezed Kiyana's tight shoulder. "Yes, they're real rats. Just, um, not from around here."

"From where?" Kiyana asked. "There's no way any rat on Earth could speak ... actual words."

"You're right," Dee said.

"Then *how* did they get here?"

Marty stepped closer and said, "Perhaps it's best you don't know. But what you should know is they want to compensate for their theft. They didn't realize how much damage they were causing you."

Chase said, "We're really sorry. We were hungry and smelled your pies baking one day while savaging through the nasty dumpsters."

Pierre nodded. "One day, we found a piece of your pie in the dumpster. Scrumptious." He drooled and wiped his mouth with the back of his paw. "And we found a way inside the shop and ate until we almost burst."

Jules rubbed his plump stomach and grinned. "While stealing is a crime, the addictiveness of your pies should be a crime in itself."

Kiyana giggled nervously and covered her mouth to suppress her growing laughter. She shook her head in disbelief. "How'd you get into the pie case after I started locking it?"

"Oh, that's Jules' doing," Pierre said. "He's picked locks for some time from where we come."

She stared at the rats, still doubtful, but she stood and walked to them. She stooped slightly and regarded each one of them. "You're so—"

Pierre crossed his forearms and pouted. "Don't call us cute."

Kiyana laughed. "So adorable!"

"That's not much better," Pierre said.

"Ignore him," Eloise said. "He's been overly grumpy lately."

Jules nodded. "Too much sugar."

Kiyana eyed them shrewdly. "So the four of you admit to stealing me pies, eh?"

The four nodded. Three of them removed their pirate hats, held them at their waists, and lowered their heads.

She looked at the Mystery Solvers. "So I owe ya a cinnamon and a Key-lime pie?"

Dee shook her head. "That's not necessary."

"Dee!" Lynn said, frowning.

"Ah, but it is," Kiyana said with a wide smile. "That's what I promised. And a promise is a promise, regardless if the outcome isn't *quite* what I expected."

Adam grinned. "And what about the rats?"

Pierre shook his head and waved his hand dismissively. "Oh, no pie for me. I couldn't possibly ... I'd rather eat something salty."

"He wasn't talking about feeding us," Eloise said. "He wanted to know what Kiyana wanted to do *to* us."

Pierre's eyes widened slightly and he blushed. "Oh, ri-i-ght. Sorry."

"I don't think they'd fit in my cooking pot too well," Kiyana said, cocking her head and holding a large rolling pin in her hands.

"That's a relief," Pierre said. A moment later, his eyes widened, his body stiffened, and he gasped. "Wait. That's a joke, right? Not about the pot's size but about cooking us?"

"Nah, I couldn't cook ya. The smell would be unbearable." Kiyana rested her hands on her hips and studied them for several long seconds. She tapped her right foot and placed an index finger to her lips. "Hmm. What do I do with da four of you?"

"Give us a pardon?" Pierre asked with a sheepish grin.

"A pardon?" Kiyana said. Her stern expression was worrisome from Dee's perspective. She couldn't imagine how the rats felt. "I'd say with the number of pies you've taken and the extra amount of work I've had to do to clean up all your messes, a pardon's out of the question."

"Oh," Pierre said.

"Due to health regulations, ya can't do anything behind the counter or in my kitchen," Kiyana said evenly.

Jules lowered to his knees and said, "Pl-l-ee-as-sss-eee, don't make us walk da plank."

Kiyana failed to keep her hardened gaze. She burst into laughter. "For one, I don't have a plank for you to walk." She wiped tears from her eyes. "And second, I could never harm any of you because—"

Pierre clamped his forepaws together, pressed them to his cheek, and cocked his head to the side. "So-o-o cute. Yeah, we know."

"Well," Kiyana said. "Ya are dat, but I was going to say dat you're different than our rats and have a higher intelligence and rationality. Maybe, ya lack a bit of conscience, though, but that can be adjusted."

Chase said, "Yes. We're willing to learn and change our ways."

"Do you 'ave a way to get back to where you came from?" she asked.

Pierre looked at Marty and shrugged.

Marty said, "No. The way they arrived here is no longer accessible."

"So ya need a place to stay, eh?" she asked them.

The four rats nodded.

"I can provide ya dat," she said. "But under one condition."

"What condition?" Dee asked.

"Perhaps they could perform a stage routine for customers?" Kiyana said.

"I don't think that would be a good idea," Marty said.

"And why *not?*" Pierre huffed. "We want to be pirates. Why not do so on stage? No threat of drowning or getting eaten by a shark. We could become famous."

Marty nodded. "Yes, in ways you never imaged. Remember when we told you what scientists do to lab rats."

Pierre stiffened. "Um, yeah?"

"Should scientists learn about you," Dee said, "they'll want to study and dissect your brains to discover *why* you have the ability to speak."

The four rats' eyes bulged with fear.

Pierre shook his head. "I'm out. Forget that."

"Not necessarily," Kiyana said.

Marty said, "What do you have in mind?"

"Well," Kiyana said. "When I saw them, one of the first things I thought was they had to be expensive, robotic toys. While not true, I could certainly tell customers dat they are. Besides, a little stage show would draw in more customers and help me regain my losses. I promise I will never put them in jeopardy, and they can live with me."

Marty and Dee exchanged glances and then nodded.

"That could work," Dee said, "if the Pie-Rats are fine with it."

Pierre drew his cutlass and pointed to the ceiling. "The show, as I've heard them say, *must* go on."

Lynn frowned at him with curiosity. "So where, exactly, have you had access to so much television?"

Eloise said, "This pie shop isn't the only place we've visited. A couple of pies lasts us several days, so we have occasionally snuck into a hotel lounge and watched television. Some of the shorter shows are drab and I'm not certain why humans need to be told they need medication all the time for things they might not have. But other than those dull flicks interrupting our movies, we sometimes get lucky and see movies about pirates and other silliness."

Dee laughed. "Those short *flicks* are commercials."

"Oh," Eloise waved her paw. "They should leave them out and allow us to enjoy the flicks instead."

"Most all humans would agree with you," Lynn said.

CHAPTER

NINETEEN

Dee smiled and listened to the four rats tell the frightening horrors they faced against the militant cats in their realm. At times, all the humans laughed while the four reenacted different escape scenarios. Their tales made her wonder about the dangers they could face haphazardly walking through a portal without any knowledge of what might be on the other side.

Kiyana held a key lime pie in one hand and a cinnamon pie in the other.

"Oh, my!" Dee said. "Those both look great."

Lynn smiled as Kiyana set the pies on the round table. Kiyana flipped the open sign to closed on the door and lowered the blinds.

"I hope they're to your liking," she said.

Pierre's cheeks puffed and he shook his head. "None for me, please."

"Ah, but I gotcha something different," Kiyana said, "since ya said dat ya don't want sweets any more."

Adam laughed with his mouth full and said, "You lost your sweet teeth?"

Pierre frowned. "Eh?"

Dee explained what it meant.

"Oh, no," Pierre said. "I'd never lose those but it'd be nice to have something a little *less* sweet from time to time."

Kiyana beamed. "Then, here ya go. Try dis one."

The pie looked like a pecan pie Dee and Marty's grandmother sometimes made during the autumn season after they all gathered bushels of pecans off the ground from under Grandpa's giant pecan trees. The only difference was the syrup covering various types of tree nuts was much darker and thicker than their grandmother's.

Dee's brow furrowed. The aroma wafted and filled her with the joy and warmth of Thanksgiving. "What is that?"

"It's a salty nut pie," Kiyana replied. "I usually don't have it on the menu, but if ya all like it, I might just add it."

"Ooh," Pierre said.

Kiyana set small plates on the table and served each of them.

The four rats tied tiny napkins around their necks and grabbed handfuls of the sticky nuts and nibbled them. The syrup coated their noses and whiskers. They closed their eyes, savoring the nutty pie.

Dee and Lynn took their phones and took pics of the rats enjoying their food. Afterwards, she and Lynn ate their pies of choice while Marty and Adam took thinner pie slices of each pie and quickly ate them.

"I want to thank all of you for helping find my pie bandits," Kiyana said. "Do you have plans for dis evening?"

Marty looked at his wristwatch.

Dee checked the time on her phone. Where had the day gone?

With reluctance in his voice, Marty said, "We'll must be leaving soon."

"At least, let me take you to a place you'll all enjoy," Kiyana said. "It's a place where even the rats will 'ave a good time."

"Does it have a beach?" Lynn asked.

"Dat it does."

CHAPTER
TWENTY

A half hour later, the Mystery Solvers were at a small inlet with a rope swing tied to a large tree. No one else was there, but the white sand and the clear, bluish water could soothe whatever ailed a person. Gentle surfing waves with white caps flowed and crashed softly near the beach.

"This is a beautiful place," Dee said.

Kiyana smiled. "Ah, it is. I like to come here to meditate. Few people trouble themselves to ever find it, but it's my place of serenity."

Lynn and Marty held hands and stood waist-deep in the water, trying to ride the shallow waves, but since the tide wasn't as strong as in other places, they didn't rise too high. They didn't seem to mind and were enjoying holding hands.

Adam waded to the shallow area where the waves broke. The four rats had abandoned their pirate clothing and left them with Dee and Kiyana on the beach. The rats surfed on flat pieces of driftwood while Adam cheered them on.

Dee took numerous pics of her brother and Lynn, Adam and the rats, and Kiyana and the surrounding beauty of the isolated inlet.

Before sunset, the rats dressed in their garb again, and Dee and Lynn took more pics of the rats in pirate poses. Everyone laughed. Everyone except Marty.

"Dee," Marty said. "We're late."

"I know. Sorry," she said. "Everyone's having such a good time."

Marty sighed. "We won't be, should our mother be looking for us."

Lynn glanced at the time on her phone and shook her head. Then she checked her messages. "Guys, my mother's on her way to your grandparents' farm. We gotta go. Now!"

TWENTY-ONE

K iyana had given them a ride back to the beach near the pier, and they quickly gave their goodbyes.

Dee felt a deep sadness and wished they could stay another week or longer. If she were Marty's age, she knew they'd be less restricted in how long they stayed somewhere. And if Marty's hint about having a wedding and a honeymoon here became reality in the future, she knew without any doubt they'd return, probably on a cruise and not through the portal.

Kiyana seemed happy to give the rats a home, and the rats were more than content to no longer have to scrounge for food or need a warm place to stay during the nights.

Dee looked at the dark recess of where the hidden portal was beneath the pier. "This is the first place I regret leaving."

"I know," Marty said.

"I agree," Lynn said. With urgency in her voice, she said, "But, if we don't get home soon, you won't be seeing me for some time. Mother will throw a fit, and I'll be grounded, if she doesn't already plan to do so."

Adam said, "Man, I'm going to miss those little guys."

"We'll be back again," Marty said, reassuringly. "But, let's go. I only hope the portal takes us home and not to a different location."

Dee's chest tightened slightly. That wasn't something she'd feared before, but since the rats had lost their portal to return home, it was possible the Mystery Solvers could end up in a strange portal loop or stranded somewhere in a future venture.

Marty grabbed Lynn's hand, and they rushed through the portal. Adam stared at the near invisible shimmering orb of the portal and took a timid step through. Dee grabbed his hand and interlocked her fingers with his. He gave her a strange look, but she shrugged and smiled slightly. She didn't grab his hand for any romantic reason, and she hoped he didn't take it that way, but she worried about the portal's stability, and should it not take them where Marty and Lynn went, at least she and Adam should arrive at the same destination. The last thing any of them needed was to end up in an unknown place ... alone.

After stepping through, she and Adam found themselves standing beside Lynn and Marty on the outskirts of her grandparents' farm. The old farm never looked more welcome and inviting than it did at that moment. Relief washed over her, and she could tell by the look in the eyes of the other three Mystery Solvers that they held the same peace of mind.

With tears shimmering in her eyes, Dee sighed. "We made it. We're home."

Lynn pointed toward the road that ran alongside the farm. "That's my mother's car. We still have time, if we hurry."

They closed and covered the portal door with brush, crossed the barbed-wire fence, and ran across the pasture. Dee and Marty's grandfather drove his UTV toward them, which startled all four of them and they stopped running.

He slowed and parked beside them.

"Thank goodness," Lynn said. "We made it just in time."

"In time? In time for what? Where have you kids been?" Grandpa asked. "You've been gone for more than two days."

The Mystery Solvers all exchanged shocked expressions.

"Two days?" Marty and Dee asked.

"You're kidding, right?" Lynn asked.

"No. Unfortunately, I'm not. Lynn, you're mother's furious," Grandpa said. "Hop in. All of ya."

Marty took the passenger seat beside Grandpa while the other three climbed into the back of the UTV.

"Why?" Lynn asked. "Mom just messaged me and said that she was on her way to pick me up. It's the first and only message—"

Lynn's phone suddenly cascaded with a flood of beeps and dialogue balloons scrolling up the screen. The messages seemed to have become more frantic as they popped up. She winced. "Change that. Sheesh! She's sent over a hundred or more messages since yesterday, but I swear, I only received the one a few minutes ago."

Lynn became paler than her normal pale. Fear darkened her eyes.

"This doesn't make any sense," Dee said to their grandfather.

Marty shook his head and tapped his wristwatch and held it to his ear. "Papaw, we've kept a close eye on the time. I promise. Dee can tell you I'm a stickler to return home before we're late."

Dee rolled her eyes. "That's an understatement."

"I don't doubt it," their grandfather replied. "However, some portals disrupt the time, or else the passage through a portal can suspend or speed time up. One can never rightly predict."

Marty frowned and took in the information. "So, you've experienced this when you traveled through the portal?"

"Many times," Grandpa replied. "But, back then, parents didn't watch your every move with vulture eyes like yours do today. Most parents didn't worry unless you were gone for several days. Kinda like you have done."

Lynn interlocked her fingers with Marty's and squeezed. Then she clasped her other hand over theirs. "I'm afraid this will be the last time I get to visit you here or at your house for a long time to come."

"Aw, now, Lynn," Grandpa said with a sympathetic grin. "Don't get all desperately depressed right yet. I bought all of you some time."

"How?" Dee asked.

"You know the old dirt road that cuts through the backside of my woods and joins the huge catfish pond between my farm and the Taylors?"

"Yes," Marty said.

"I told all of your mothers and Gramms that you're helping Ol' Man Taylor clear the brush from around his fishing cottage at the edge of the catfish pond," Grandpa said.

Dee thought it funny that Grandpa would refer to his neighbor as an old man when the two men went to high school together decades earlier. She wondered if Grandpa was referred to as an old man by the Taylor family.

Grandpa said, "I told them after a long day's work, all of you planned to catch catfish from the small pond and cook them over a campfire and camp in the cottage overnight."

"No offense, but if I stayed overnight unsupervised with Marty, my mother would have my throat," Lynn said. "Or worse, she'd send me to a convent."

Grandpa laughed. "Don't get yourself fitted for a nun's habit just yet."

"I don't plan to. Never. No way," Lynn said. Her eyes widened with hope. "But why's that?"

"I told them I was helping all of you and staying the nights, too, which I did against Gramms' wishes."

"Thanks, Papaw," Marty said.

"For *lying*?" Grandpa shook his head and snickered. "Don't forget that when you lie, eventually, the truth will catch up to you, and sometimes you pay a hefty price in a different manner. And boy, have I *ever*."

Adam eased up in the backseat and said, "What happened?"

"Ol Man Taylor's place near the cottage is overgrown with weeds and crawling with—"

"Snakes?" Adam asked.

"Poison ivy!" Grandpa said, scratching his stomach through his buttoned shirt. "Now, I saw a few kingsnakes but no venomous snakes. But Taylor's place is covered with poison ivy and just to get to the steps to the cottage's porch, I had to use a garden hoe to yank down the vines. And now, I have itches in my britches in places I never would've hoped to itch or get stitches. Calamine is a Godsend, though, and I guess we should invest in a few bottles of it."

Dee winced.

"We?" Marty asked.

Adam held up a long vine he found in the back floorboard of the UTV. It had leaves of three. His eyes widened. "Wait. You mean *this*?"

Grandpa nodded. "Yep. I thought I'd bring you a small vine of poison ivy to help you identify it."

"We know how to identify it, Papaw. You *know* that. Sheesh!" Dee gasped. "Leaves of three, leave them be. Adam, *why* would you pick it up?"

"I just thought it was an ordinary vine," Adam said. "Then, I saw the three leaves—"

"Why would anyone put poison ivy in the UTV?" Marty asked, looking over his shoulder at Lynn, Dee, and Adam.

Grandpa said, "A gentle reminder never hurts."

Dee and Lynn edged to their side of the backseat, trying to ensure they didn't touch any of the leaves.

Dee frowned. "It seems like you *want* us to get poison ivy?"

"Well," Grandpa said, "if you want to sell your story and have me *lie* about your whereabouts for the past two days, I can't be the only one with a poison ivy rash, now can I?"

Lynn didn't hesitate and ripped off one of the leaves. She rubbed it on her left wrist and left calf.

Marty frowned. "Why'd you do that?"

"It's a small price to pay." She grinned at him. "Trust me. I'd rather itch for a week or so and be able to see you than not itch and be locked in my bedroom every day until my mother comes home from work. You might think I'm being melodramatic, but I'm not."

Grandpa laughed and shook his head. "Young love makes one do strange things."

Lynn offered the leaf to Marty.

Reluctantly, Marty sighed and took the leaf. He rubbed the leaf on his calves. Then Dee did the same.

"Ahh!" Adam said. "Help, guys!"

The long poison ivy vine somehow coiled and looped around Adam's neck. The more he tried to free himself, the more tangled he became.

Grandpa slowed and parked the UTV at the pasture gate and grimaced. "Ooh. That's not good. Hold on, son, and I'll help ya."

Grandpa hurried around to where Adam was seated. Wearing thick gardening gloves, he took a pair of pliers and snipped the vine in several places. "Only you could do this, Adam."

"In my defense," Adam said, "*I* didn't put it in the UTV."

"Curious kills the—"

"Re-o-oow!" Pywackett said, appearing on the ground near Grandpa's feet.

Grandpa jumped slightly. "That dag-gone cat's gonna give me a heart attack some day."

Dee jumped out of the UTV and grabbed Pywackett. The black cat purred. "He missed us!"

Grandpa took the pieces of the poison ivy vine and tossed them on a pile of old brush he'd eventually burn. "Where'd the portal take you this time?"

"Jamaica," Dee said.

Grandpa's eyes widened. "Really?"

The Mystery Solvers nodded.

"I thought I smelled salt water and ... a hint of cinnamon? I definitely smell sunscreen." He looked at Lynn. "You'll have to tell me all about it when your mothers and Gramms aren't around."

"Sure," Dee said. "We took a lot of pics on our phones."

Grandpa took off his hat and wiped his brow with a handkerchief. "I'd love to see them. Unlikely you found any mysteries while you were there."

Dee chuckled. "Actually, you'll have a difficult time believing *what* we solved."

"Doubtful. I've yet to tell you about some of the strange things I've encountered before the four of you were yet a thought," Grandpa said.

Marty's expression became somber. "I'd love to hear them. But we learned something today, too."

"What's that?" Grandpa asked, before pointing to Adam. "Undo the gate, would you, Adam?"

"Sure," Adam said.

Dee loved how her grandfather made Adam feel welcomed and wanted since Adam had not seen his father in years. Her grandfather knew Adam's home situation, and she guessed Grandpa sought to encourage and bond with Adam. Adam had become more open and optimistic during the two years he'd been a part of Dee's Mystery Solvers.

Marty treated Adam more like a brother than a younger friend, and this, too, had built Adam's self-esteem. They trained together in boxing and martial arts and played catch or tossed the football on Saturdays before the college games began.

All of this had brought a maturity to Adam, and was probably a big reason his deductive reasoning had increased while solving this Pie-Rats mystery. Lynn had noticed, and Dee had as well. Adam no longer second-guessed himself. Being including in Dee and Marty's family, as well as the club, had given Adam the comfort of fitting in and belonging. Something he'd not had before becoming their friend.

Grandpa faced Marty. "What'd ya learn?"

"Have you ever known two portals to overlap?" Marty asked.

Grandpa adjusted his hat, frowned, and shook his head slightly. "No, why?"

"Two portals must've overlapped beneath the pier in Ochos Rios," Marty said. "But what's scarier is the second portal somehow vanished or collapsed, leaving the ones who came through it stranded in Jamaica. They said that it had been destroyed."

"I'll be," Grandpa said. "That *is* disturbing."

"It is," Dee said.

Grandpa got back into the driver's seat of the UTV. "Until we think this through, perhaps you shouldn't travel through the portal again. At least for a while."

Dee nodded. "I agree. Besides, we have a lot more important things to attend to."

"Oh?" Grandpa asked. He motioned Adam to push the gate wider and after driving through, he waited for Adam to shut the gate and get into the UTV. "Like what?"

"The clubhouse, for one," Dee said.

"How's your clubhouse coming along?" Grandpa asked. "That will take some time to clean, eh?"

"Yes. We haven't gotten much done."

"Why not?"

"Still working out some of the kinks," Dee said.

"What kind of kinks?"

"It's, uh ... a little bit haunted."

Grandpa feigned a pseudo, wide-eyed look of terror. "Haunted?"

Marty nodded.

Grandpa gave him a shrewd stare. "What have you seen?"

"Several ghosts," Marty said. "Some of them aren't too happy with our arrival."

"You should smudge the place."

Dee sighed. "We tried."

"Tried?" Lynn said. "We never got to actually attempt smudging. And I've never experienced such resistance from ghosts before, either."

"Yep. It only made them madder," Marty said.

"Ah, I see. Maybe you should consider something else," Grandpa said. "Find a better place for a clubhouse."

"That's what I suggested many times," Adam said.

"Coward," Lynn said, sticking her tongue out at him.

Adam frowned. His face reddened. "I'm not a coward. That's the spookiest place I've ever been. It's worse than the Tangled Forest. Marty can see ghosts, but I know they're in that old manor because they throw things at me or try to shove me down the stairs."

"Really, Papaw? Find a better place?" Dee said. "That's the perfect place. All those overgrown shrubs and massive cedar trees, plus the old, creepy, granite tombstones ... It's highly unlikely anyone would dare sneak into the manor."

"You did, though," Grandpa said with a wide smile. "Right?"

"Of course," Dee said. "I've always been—"

"A bit prying," Grandpa said, looking at her in the mirror.

Dee's mouth gaped and she faced Lynn in disbelief.

Grandpa laughed. "You know it's truth and being nosey is what makes an investigator even better than the normal sleuth. While it definitely aids you, it can also be dangerous. Curiosity blinds us to our surroundings sometimes."

Dee sighed. "You're right. I make bold decisions sometimes without thinking a situation through."

"At least you don't duck and run away," Lynn said.

"I realize that's a poke at Adam, Lynn," Grandpa said. "But sometimes you need to run or you'll die. It's just that simple. Especially when you're dealing with the paranormal. Remember that. If it's your survival on the line, hightail it to safety, lest you become a ghost yourself. But what Adam said alarms me. If they're bent on harming you, maybe you should find a different place."

Dee shook her head vigorously. "No. I'm telling you. The old manor is the best place."

"Minus the ghosts," Adam said.

"I agree," Marty nodded.

"Hmm," Grandpa said. "If smudging didn't work, and you're too stubborn to find another place, there's really only one thing you can do."

"What's that?" Dee asked.

"Ask the ghosts what they want," he said. "Marty's the only one who sees and speaks to them. So, he'll have to find out what they need."

"Basically," Lynn said. "You're saying they have unfinished business, and that's why they won't leave?"

Grandpa nodded. "In a manner of speaking."

He stopped the UTV at the back porch and turned in his seat so he could see all of them. "After supper tonight, I want to see your pictures. I've always wanted to take Gramms to Jamaica."

Dee shot Marty a quick glance and smiled. "Perhaps you will someday."

"I doubt it," he said. "We're too old now."

"You never know," Dee said.

Grandpa shook his head. "If I were to take Gramms through the portal, the whole world would discover *our* secret portal. Her lips flap worse than a flag in a tornado. She can't keep secrets and *loves* to gossip. You *know* she wouldn't keep it to herself."

Dee giggled. "You don't have to take her through the portal. You could go on a cruise to Jamaica."

"A cruise?" he frowned. "At our ages, *why* would we take a cruise?"

"Because, Papaw," Dee said, "it would be a romantic thing to do for her."

Grandpa watched as Lynn took Marty's hand and looked into his eyes. Her affection for Marty beamed.

Grandpa's eyes widened, and he harshly cleared his throat. "Oooh. Look, you two. You're too young to even be considering marriage yet. Come on. I better get the four of you to the front so your mothers and Gramms can look ya over."

He drove the UTV around to the front of the farmhouse where Gramms sat on the porch swing. Glenda and Terri sat on the opposite porch swing. The Mystery Solvers got out of the vehicle and Grandpa drove to the shed behind the house where he kept the UTV.

Gramms grinned. "I thought you kids had decided to rough it for the rest of your lives."

Dee smiled and shook her head. "No. Not us."

Glenda gave them a shrewd look. "You certainly look like ya'll ran through a wood chipper. Anyone else, other than your Papaw, get themselves into poison ivy?"

They all nodded. To Dee's surprise, small blistering welts were already forming on their skin where they'd rubbed the leaves. That seemed abnormally fast, given that less than five minutes had passed.

Terri shook her head and pointed a stern finger at Dee and Marty. "See what happened? If you'd have gone to the festival, you wouldn't have gotten into a patch of poison ivy. Not saying you deserve it, but—"

Dee huffed. "We're sorry, Mom. Really, we are. But, to be honest, I never wanted to go to the festival."

"Ah," Terri said. "The truth comes out."

"You didn't ask if we wanted to go," Dee said. "You insisted. You might enjoy it, but it bores me. How'd it go anyway?"

"Fine," Terri said. "Glenda came along, so ..."

Glenda winked at Dee. "I'm with you, girl. B-O-R-I-N-G!"

"Hey!" Terri said with a frown. "You said that you were having a *great* time."

"Was I on my phone when I said it?" Glenda asked.

"When are you *not*?"

Glenda laughed. "Whenever the boss comes into the room or when something of great interest captures me, I abandoned it. But, I was trying to get in touch with Lynn. I tried the entire time we were at the festival."

Dee leaned close to Lynn's ear and whispered, "Probably why you have one hundred messages, huh?"

Lynn crossed her arms. "No doubt, but probably more than that."

Adam shook his shirt and rubbed his neck where the vine had looped around him.

"Oh, dear," Gramms said. "Don't start scratching."

Adam pulled off his shirt and halfway growled. He was covered with welts around his neck and down his arms. "Ahh, I can't help it. It itches so badly."

Terri held up a drugstore bag. "We got some Calamine lotion on our way here. Be careful not to scratch any blisters or you'll spread the rash."

Adam's eyes watered. "I got it *all* over me."

"Why didn't you kids get back to the house sooner?" Glenda asked.

Grandpa peered around the corner of the house and met Dee's gaze. He put an index finger to his lips, which didn't hide his gentle smile.

"We got kinda busy," Dee said.

Marty nodded. "The cottage near the pond was a mess."

Gramms eased off the porch swing and opened the screen door. "I'll go check on supper while your mothers put lotion on your rashes."

Adam's mother had not come, nor had she called, Dee later learned. His face saddened.

"Don't worry," Dee said. "My mother will put lotion on you."

"Thanks," Adam said with a slight smile.

TWENTY-TWO

After supper, the Mystery Solvers sat on the back porch with Grandpa. All five of them were covered with Calamine lotion. Dee flipped through the pics on her phone, showing him the four rats dressed like pirates.

"And here's one," Dee said, "of Eloise and Chase trying to surf on pieces of driftwood."

Grandpa laughed. "These little guys traveled through a different portal than you?"

Marty nodded. "As best as we can tell."

"Hmm. Strange that theirs was destroyed," he said. "By *talking* cats with tanks?"

"Re-o-ow!" Pywackett appeared at Grandpa's feet.

"Dagnabbit!" Grandpa said, jumping out of his rocking chair.

Dee, Marty, Lynn, and Adam all laughed.

After a few seconds, Grandpa smiled. "Can't you put a bell or something on him to warn an old man before the cat appears?"

Marty sighed. "We've tried. The problem is, the bell rings in the place where he transports from. The sound cannot precede his arrival. Even magic cannot escape the laws of physics."

Grandpa said, "I'd argue that, if I *knew* the laws of physics. Pure, unadulterated magic defies logic and science, which is why for centuries people in high positions around the world wanted to eradicate its existence."

"Don't I know it," Lynn said.

"Its use might've gone underground, into hiding, but that didn't make it weaker. It's actually stronger," Grandpa said.

Dee frowned. "And you know this how?"

Grandpa cocked a brow and looked around to ensure Gramms wasn't at the door or near one of the windows. "Need you really ask with all the strange things you encountered so far? The Tangled Forest, Pywackett, and the portal? Magic has been hidden for so long, it's prying its way through to the surface. While Marty might feel cursed that he sees ghosts, it's really a blessing in some ways."

Marty said, "How?"

"Ghosts and spirits stand between us and the afterlife. Or, I should say, the ghosts that have not passed through to the other side. They know things we cannot possibly see or hear, but you, you can talk to them. They can tell you things. Understand?"

Marty nodded.

"These ghosts at the new clubhouse you have, while some might be dangerous, others might hold keys of knowledge to what's about to happen," Grandpa said. "But tread lightly. Very, very lightly. Some secrets aren't meant to be revealed. Ravenswood, for whatever reason, has a portal. The portal's here for a reason. I was foolish to try to hide it when I was about your ages. Worse things might yet come to the surface, and perhaps I prevented that from happening for a while. Who knows? But never go into the portal alone. *Ever.* Only time will tell. Until then, stick close together and anything you discover, please don't keep it from me. I may be old, but I can still help you."

The evening breeze brushed over them. Dee shivered. Her attention went toward the narrow strip of trees where the hidden portal awaited. What waited for them on the other side the next time they entered? What sought to pass through now?

She swallowed hard. Denial of magic was no longer an option, and Lynn had been devoting extra hours into her paranormal research and specifically studying witchcraft.

Each of the Mystery Solvers held an important role. Marty and Lynn understood theirs. Adam was still mentally maturing and growing less afraid. Dee had no idea what her role was, but she didn't think it'd be too long before she discovered what part she played. After all, she was the one that started their club and she loved to solve mysteries. She wondered if this mystery would cost them all too much. Only time could reveal it. Until then, she'd be watchful. Ever watchful.

THE END

NEXT IN SERIES:

THE NEW CLUBHOUSE

ABOUT THE AUTHOR

Leonard D. Hilley II was a quiet, shy kid with an inquisitive mind. Learning to read at an early age, he fell in love with books. He read every book he could get his hands on and stacks of dark comics about ghosts, monsters, and creepy things that stalk the night.

Like a lot of boys, he caught beetles, wooly bears, butterflies, and had an ant farm. When he was ten, his interests in science increased even more after seeing a professor's insect collection. Soon he set out on his quest to build his own collection. He also learned to rear butterflies and moths to obtain perfect specimens. He learned botany, gardening, and set his goal to become an entomologist.

At eleven, he watched Star Wars. His imagination soared. Soon after, he discovered Roger Zelazny's Chronicles of Amber. During this time, he wrote the first draft of a novel. A novel he later discarded, but the characters stuck with him. Years later, these characters came to life in Shawndirea, which Hilley intended to be a novella for Devils Den. The characters, however, refused to be ignored and took the opportunity to unveil Aetheaon in their first epic fantasy. Lady Squire: Dawn's Ascension was quick to follow.

Shawndirea was Hilley's farewell to butterfly collecting, and those who have read the novel understand why. He has taken Ray Bradbury's advice to heart: "Follow the characters." He does. He follows, listens, and take notes—often never knowing where these characters are going to take him, but he's never been disappointed in the results.

Hilley earned a B.S. in Biology and an MFA in Creative Writing to combine his love of science and writing.

Sci-fi Titles: Predators of Darkness: Aftermath, Beyond the Darkness, The Game of Pawns, Death's Valley, and The Deimos Virus.

Epic Fantasy: Shawndirea (Aetheaon Chronicles: Book One), Lady Squire (Aetheaon Chronicles: Book Two), Frosthammer (Aetheaon Chronicles: Book Three), Shadowfae (Aetheaon Chronicles: Book Four), and Devils Den.

UF/PR: Succubus: Shadows of the Beast (Nocturnal Trinity Series: Book One), Raven (Nocturnal Trinity Series: Book Two), and A Touch of the Familiar (Nocturnal Trinity Series: Book Three).

YA UF/Paranormal: Forrest Wollinsky Vampire Hunter; Forrest Wollinsky: Blood Mists of London; Forrest Wollinsky: Predestined Crossroads.

Dee's Mystery Solvers: The Beating Heart Beneath Hollow Hill Cemetery, Buried Treasure, Witch Cat, The Portal, The New Clubhouse, and The Pie-rats of the Caribbean.